110679773

ROGUE RIVER

Gold had been discovered where the Rogue and Illinois Rivers spilled into the Pacific. Miners' shacks lined the beach and the town of Sebastopol steadily grew on the banks of the twin rivers in back. The nearest Army Post was thirty miles away at Crescent City, but no one worried much. The area was fairly peaceful.

Luke Prine made his journey into Crescent City once a week carrying gold dust and mail—and then Luke got a warning.

Someone had been trading guns for Indian girls— and that meant trouble on two counts.

But no one cared to listen—until it was too late.

ROGUE RIVER

Chad Merriman

First published by New English Library 1963

This hardback edition 2000
by Chivers Press
by arrangement with
Golden West Literary Agency

ISBN 0 7540 8107 9

British Library Cataloguing in Publication Data available

Printed and bound in Great Britain by
Redwood Books, Trowbridge, Wiltshire

1   THE MORNING was kitten-new when Luke Prine arrived at the cabin of Jug-Up Johnson on the edge of Sebastopol. He had been inland and, coming back across the mountains, he had learned something that disturbed his few hours of sleep at his ranch, now some four miles behind him. So he had cleaned up, saddled a fresh horse, and ridden on down to the mining camp, hoping to get the answer to an upsetting question.

Jug-Up's cabin was beside the river trail with a view of the Rogue, grown wider and calmer here where it was about to spill into the Pacific. Luke reined in, seeing before him a structure of logs, poorly built and, from its appearance, never once repaired. To the left was a shed where a cow was kept, and between it and the cabin there was a little chicken yard. Wood was piled in the dooryard, with a chopping block beside the steps. The door was shut, but smoke wisped up from the mud chimney to show industry indoors that, Luke knew, wouldn't be Jug-Up's.

The door opened before he had swung down. It was Jody who looked out, Jug-Up's daughter, the only family the man had. She stared at Luke's tall, hard-muscled figure, then with shy uncertainty responded to the grin on his weathered face.

"Howdy, Jody," Luke said warmly, for of her he had a high opinion. "Your pa home?"

She shook her head, but he swung down anyway, and when he turned he noticed the smudge of flour on the side of her nose. She was a plain girl compared to some, although slim built and tiny at the waist. She didn't say anything.

"See you're bakin'," he encouraged.

Jody found her tongue finally to say, "Reckon I am."

He had shown no great astuteness, for it was a safe bet

5

that, any time of day, she'd be found at her endless toil. He'd talked to a man who told him her father was never out of debt to Pete Latta, the man he worked for when he was sober, Latta simply applying his wages to Jug-Up's whiskey bill. So during the three years Jody had lived here she had baked and sold to the miners: bread, pies, cakes, and sometimes fancier pastries. The cow was her acquisition, and so were the chickens. It was scratch for herself or go hungry, since she couldn't live on gouge-eye the way her father did.

Jody hadn't asked him in, but when Luke started up the steps she moved back, and he followed her into the cabin. It was clean but without much else to recommend it, a big fireplace with a Dutch oven, a work table against a wall, an eating table in the center of the room, and a lean-to for sleeping. She'd been working dough, as had been highly indicated by the flour on her little nose.

She said hesitantly, "Had your breakfast?"

He was no stranger here, for he understood her loneliness and had stopped by when he could for a little talk and coffee and a sample of her baking. It struck him that such visits had grown infrequent since last summer, when Judge Kelly's niece came to Sebastopol, although it was not probable that Jody would notice.

"Had a bite," Luke admitted, "but if there's coffee on the crane, it'd go good with whatever you've baked lately."

She smiled finally, and when she did so her face was downright pretty. She poured a cup of coffee, a strong girl and swift-moving. She lifted an overturned milk pan and cut him a third of the dried peach pie that had been hidden under it. But suddenly he wasn't watching, for he could hear snoring from the next room. Jody always said Jug-Up was gone or sick abed, never admitting it when he was plain senseless from booze. Which he was right now, and that proved his credit at Pete Latta's had recently been extended.

Jody saw he had heard, and she flushed but offered no excuses, going back to her work. Luke sat down at the table where she had put his pie and coffee, his face dark, the troublesome question answered.

Just at dark the previous evening he had come onto Silver Creek Prairie, on the Illinois, and the camp of a friendly Indian where he had left a horse the week before on his way to the interior. The confluence of the Illinois and Rogue had been just ahead of him, dangerous country because of its proximity to the stronghold of the hostile Indians who for the past four months had been off the reservation. The friendly Indian's name was Bearpaw, and he liked white people and had no truck with the "bad Injuns" that now roamed the mountains. Luke knew something bothered him, but Bearpaw didn't divulge it until just before Luke headed on down the river.

"White man come up river." Bearpaw crooked an arm, lifted it at the elbow and made a gurgling sound in his throat. Luke knew that he meant Jug-Up. "Go to bad Injun camp. Pack ponies." Bearpaw held up three fingers to show how many ponies. "Maybe trade guns for squaws for jig-jig house."

"Pete Latta's deadfall?" Luke's eyes had bugged. "That how he gets Injun girls to work in his stinkin' place?"

"Injuns want plenty guns. Good gun worth bad squaw anytime."

"You sure?"

"Bearpaw hear, no see . . ."

Luke no longer enjoyed his pie, although Jody could make dried peaches taste fresh, and her crusts were rich and flaky. Jug-Up's sodden noises in the lean-to proved what Bearpaw had hinted, at least that Jug-Up had gone into the mountains for Latta. But Luke wasn't going to lay that shame on Jody by telling her what he had heard. He wouldn't be able to question Jug-Up, but he would take the matter up with Latta, himself.

He heard Jody say, "They tell me you went over the range," and it struck him that she always had a good idea of his doings. Being in the express business, he was never long in one place. "Where to now?"

"Missed a trip to Crescent City," Luke said. "Reckon I'll crack out for there in the morning."

Jody cocked her head. "Hear there's a dance at Big Flat, day after tomorrow night. You be back in time for it?"

"Dance? Hadn't heard of it. You going? The boys'd admire to have you there, Jody." This coast country was extremely shy on women.

She said nothing, and he turned down the offer of more pie. Jug-Up was still snoring earnestly in the lean-to, but Luke let Jody's claim that he was away ride the way she preferred. He thanked her for the refreshment, said he hoped to see her at the dance, and went out to his horse. He didn't feel good. He had to take the lid off a stinking kettle of fish, and the stench was bound to affect her.

He stared at the river flowing below him, an extremely long river already storied with a history of bloody violence. There were two gorges by which it escaped the inland valleys and broke through to the Pacific, gorges that joined on this

7

isolated, thinly populated side of the mountains. He had followed the Illinois on his mission inland because the main stem, the Rogue, was cut off, converted into an impregnable mountain fortress by the hostile Indians. These were upper river Indians whose valleys had been taken over by miners and settlers. They had fought bitterly until overcome and confined to the reservation they had again left. Luke shook his head and rode on down the river toward the town.

Sebastopol was scattered through the trees in the rounded right angle formed by sea and river on the south bank of the Rogue. Its fifty or sixty cabins stood where it had occurred to the builders to place them, and the one effort at order was in the main street whose sandy soil was now stabilized and hardened by the winter rains. Face to face along this short avenue were the merchandising firms of Huntley & O'Brien, Jno. & Augustus Upton, Pratt & Blake, and H. I. Gerow. The Gold Beach Hotel stood at the south end. And on out the California trail were the barn and warehouse of F. H. Pratt, who ran a pack- and saddle-train to Crescent City, the all-weather port sixty miles south.

Out the road on the north end of town, built against the river bank, was the wharf where the sloop "Gold Beach," owned by Huntley & O'Brien, was tied up for the winter. At a berth upstream was the schooner "Rambler," owned by Pratt & Blake, also waiting until the winds stood fair again for San Francisco. This would not occur until summer, and at other seasons the bar was too dangerous to cross.

These features shaped the town, and squeezed in the spaces between the larger structures were shops of a carpenter and tinsmith who also was a barber, an apothecary who doubled as doctor and dentist, and a butcher who sold salmon from the river and beef and pork when he could obtain it from the settlers. Such space as remained was occupied by the town's half dozen saloons, billiard parlors and gambling houses, a couple of eating houses smaller than the hotel's dining room, and the office of Judge Patrick Kelly, Attorney At Law.

Swinging onto Main Street from the river trail, Luke aimed his horse for the hitchrack in front of the judge's office. The street was mainly deserted, it being too early for the settlers from Big Flat to be coming down the river by boat or saddlehorse to trade and much too early for the miners from the river bars and beach placers, by far the dominant element, who made the town roar by night. Thus depopulated, Sebastopol looked especially vulnerable to the several hun-

8

dred vengeance-hungry warriors hardly thirty miles away in the mountains.

When he entered the big, plain room of the law office, it was to find the lawyer standing by his heating stove, a cigar in his fingers, a moody look on his lean, bearded face. A tall man, Kelly wore a frayed frock coat and checked pants with baggy knees. The whole room evidenced his lack of prosperity in the two years he had been in Sebastopol, where there was little law business although the region had finally been formed into Curry County.

Kelly said forlornly, "Howdy," and shook hands. "I see by your look that you didn't get anywhere."

"Well, I got there and back," Luke said, "but that's about it."

Since riding the wild trails was his occupation, he had been asked by Kelly and some of the other more responsible citizens of the beach country to make his way through the Indian zone and try to talk sense into the heads of the authorities on the other side. When in October, four months ago, the Indians went off the reservation near the Rogue headwaters, Oregon Territory had authorized and raised a whole regiment of militia, totaling over nine hundred men. This force had done so poorly that, after driving the Indians into the Rogue gorge and plugging its upper end, it had gone into winter quarters to await a spring still several months in the future.

Luke had called attention to the fact that the Indians had been pushed down on top of the coast country, whose protection had been officially ignored. Since militia companies tripped over each other, inland, and there were four companies of army regulars idling at Fort Lane, in the same vicinity, he had suggested that two or three companies might be spared. If they could slip down the Illinois and plug the lower end of the stronghold, the coast citizens would be much relieved.

"Seen the volunteer colonel," Luke told Kelly. "He's busy building himself headquarters at Forest Dale, clean across the county from the Injuns. Said we're outta his jurisdiction, anyhow. The officer at Fort Lane listened to me, but he's got orders from the Pacific Department to stay put and get ready for next spring."

"By which time," Kelly said, "there might not be anything left of us worth saving."

"That's what I tried to get across, but they say we'll have to raise our own militia or look to Fort Orford and Fort Humboldt." Luke's mouth twisted. They had tried putting

9

their own militia at Big Bend, below the stronghold, thirty men organized under Johnny Poland, without official sanction and so without pay or even rations. A few weeks of it, and they had pulled back and disbanded. As to the army forts, Humboldt was eighty miles south in California, garrisoned by fifty men, while Orford was thirty miles north with a roster of twenty-five men. "And it might be worse than we thought," Luke resumed. "An old Injun in the mountains dropped a broad hint that somebody's runnin' guns in there."

Kelly's eyes sharpened. "My God. Who?"

Luke shook his head. "Sorry, but I'd as soon not say till I've got more than an old buck's say-so. Which I intend to get."

The judge fingered his whiskers as if they had started to itch. "Well, you'd better tell the Indian agent."

"I aim to."

"And come over to the house for supper, this evening."

Luke had hoped for such an invitation. Kelly had had him meet his niece in Crescent City, she arriving there by schooner from San Francisco the previous summer, and escort her to Sebastopol where she was to live with the Kellys. Going down the coast, Luke had dreaded the job, not being at ease with most women. But one look at Carol Dennis, and he was of a different frame of mind. Since then, he had seen as much of her as she and the Kellys would permit.

He said, "Thank you kindly, if it's not a bother," and went out.

He stood pondering on the sidewalk a moment afterward. Lattaville was a half mile down the California trail, a stinkhole of shacks and cabins grown up around Pete Latta's deadfall. The place rocked on its foundations from early evening until early morning but at other times was quiet as a graveyard. There was little chance of finding Latta up and about at this early hour.

The Indian agent had a cabin near a fishing village of peaceful Rogues, not far up the river. Luke decided to see him and go on home and get ready for his trip to Crescent City. He would come in early enough that evening to ask Latta a few pointed questions before he went to Kelly's house for supper.

He rode back up the river, not seeing Jody Johnson again when he went past her cabin. He crossed Indian Creek, rode by Elephant Rock and then the ferry, and finally forded Trashberry Creek, on the upper length of which he had his own land claim where he kept the horses he used in his business. The Indian village was in a bend of the river, about half a mile farther on. As he rode on toward it, Luke reflected that the Indian superintendent had made an undiplomatic choice when he appointed Ben Wright the local agent. Luke knew from experience.

He had not been in the West very long when he discovered that his own bent was neither for mining nor tilling the land. He had a feeling for country, with far places always tempting him, and after a bitter winter on the placer bars of California he had hired out to Cram, Rogers & Co., northern agents for the big Adams Express. For three years he had covered the trails between Sacramento and Yreka, up near the Oregon border, and the scores of intervening mining camps spawned by the Gold Rush.

Ben Wright had been mining near Yreka then, living with a squaw even while advertising himself as an Indian fighter of great prowess. And he'd proved his boasts, leading a volunteer company onto the desert east of Yreka to chastise a band of Modocs who were plaguing the emigrant trail from the East. He'd taught them a lesson. With a great show of friendliness, he invited the suspected band to a feast and powwow at his camp, claiming the Great White Father in Washington had sent him to make them his friends and children. And while the Modocs were gorging themselves on beef he had thoughtfully provided, their arms left outside the camp at his insistence, Wright's volunteers had caught up their own rifles and started making good Indians. Only three or four out of about fifty Indians lived through it, and there were women and children among the newly manufactured good ones.

Afterward Wright led his company back to Yreka, scalps dripping from rifle barrels and horses' bridles, and the town put on a banquet for them at the hotel. Ben became known as Captain Wright, and he somehow wangled a job with the Indian Department and eventually arrived at Sebastopol. If he thought the local Indians didn't know and resent his victory, he was as crazy as he was vainglorious. Somehow they always heard about such things, and they never forgot them.

Luke had come over the mountains ahead of Wright, starting as soon as he heard of the new gold strikes on the coast of northern California and southern Oregon, a bulge in the coast that constituted the westernmost point in the nation. He remembered hearing a man say, the day the news hit Yreka, "This side of the Missouri you're west, and this side of the Rockies you're far west. But over there, mister, you're west as all hell, and that's where I hanker to get myself." It had struck Luke the same way, and he had set up in the express business for himself over here, running between the new mining country and Crescent City. . . .

Wright was standing in his dooryard when Luke rode in through the river trees to his cabin, a man whose physical stature didn't live up to his self-opinion. The Indian who stood with him was Enos, a stray from Canada who had come into the country with General Fremont. Deserting while Fremont helped take California from the Mexicans, Enos had made his home with the coast Rogues. Highly intelligent, he was friendly with the whites and had lived with them enough to speak their language. Since he passed freely among the peaceful lower Rogues, having a wife in the village below Big Bend, and was equally at home with the Chetcos, Pistols, Euchres and Three Sisters, Wright relied upon him heavily for information about his charges.

"Howdy thar, Luke," Wright said jovially. "Light down and rest your piles."

"Kind of pressed." Luke looked uncertainly at Enos, then told the agent what he had learned from Bearpaw, again neglecting to name the accused gunrunner for Jody's sake. "I got a feeling there's something to it, Ben. If the army people in San Francisco could be convinced, they might send us a few more troops."

Wright seemed incredulous, but he glanced questioningly at Enos, who shook his head derisively.

"Bearpaw big liar," Enos said in his deep voice. "Injuns no like Bearpaw, so Bearpaw no like Injuns and all the time tell lies."

"It shore sounds tall, Luke," Wright agreed. "More like spite than fact."

Luke was willing to be reassured, but he couldn't dismiss it as lightly as Wright had. The whites liked Enos, since he was friendly and peaceful, but there was something sleek and mysterious about him, too. "On the other hand," Luke rejoined, "we'll wake up with our scalps gone some morning if our Injuns dig up the hatchet and join the hostiles. That's what the hostiles want, and they've got plenty of guns for themselves. If they're buying more, it could be to arm recruits."

Wright snorted. "That old buck's buggered you, Luke. Enos'd know if anything like that was goin' on."

The Indian nodded importantly.

Luke realized he would have to cut the deck deeper to get the agent to listen and use such powers as he had to obtain better protection for the coast. "Well, I hoped I wouldn't have to mention names, Ben. What I heard is that Pete Latta swaps guns for Injun girls to work in his cribs. Jug-Up Johnson was in the stronghold with three pack ponies the other day. I was at Jug-Up's cabin a while ago, and he's sleepin' one off. It kind of makes sense, Ben. He's earned some money somehow. Latta's been here a long time, so it might have gone on a long time, with the coast Injuns armed a lot better than we've figured."

Wright scratched his whiskers, not wanting to believe it. "Enos, you hear anything about woman swappin'?" he asked.

Enos shook his head.

Wright said, "The old buck told you a purty good yarn, Luke, but that's all it is. Forget it."

"I hope you're right," Luke said and rode off toward his claim.

2   WHERE THE TRAIL crossed the south point of the Rogue estuary and came in against the beach at Lattaville, weathered by oceanic winds and rains and bleached by salt and sunshine. Pete Latta's saloon, casino and bordello, nested among the rocks and twisted evergreens, extended its log-walled rear compound to the blow sand, with its front and entrance on the trail. On its flanks and beyond the trail were a score of ill-built, ill-kept buildings, Latta's stable and storehouses and the domiciles of men who worked for Latta or simply found the location more to their gamy taste than Sebastopol.

Pete Latta stood at the window of his second-floor room, which commanded a view of the miners toiling in the region immediately adjacent to his establishment. He was a tall, thin, dark man of thirty-five whose nervous energies robbed him of repose. Because of the sandy underfooting of the areas he haunted, he wore heavy leather boots, but into their tops were tucked trousers of expensive dark cloth. He wore linen that was always spotless, starched and ironed, and even in the heat of one of his all-night games he refused to follow the practice of removing coats. There was an impeccable vanity about him, a pride of person and a compulsive avoidance of what he deemed to be unclean.

Latta ignored the first rap on his door, as fixed a rule as that which kept his closest associates from entering his private quarters unannounced. Below him on the beach and extending north and south as far as he could see was one of the earliest mining operations in the region, taking place from the edge of the restless surf to the cliffs above the dry sand.

Gold Beach, they called the general area, which term had grown to include the placer bars found up the Rogue as far as the mountains and on all the lesser streams tumbling into the Pacific. During its life, a goodly share of Gold Beach's output had gone into his own pocket. He'd seen to it, having arrived with the first excited horde drawn to the lonely country by the black, gold-bearing sands washed up from the deep. Just as the miners had learned to extract the tricky, fine-grained treasure with carpet-lined sluices or plates of copper coated with quicksilver, he had worked out methods of extracting the bulk of it from them.

From his window he could see into the walled compound behind his main building, attached to it on the principle of the old trading posts. Butted to the walls, all around the inside, were long low buildings divided into cramped rooms. Here was plied the oldest profession, his strongest puller and biggest money maker, for this was almost entirely a country of men without their own women. His patrons might ignore the bar and gaming tables, but few could resist the shapely, dusky, modest-mannered girls to be seen moving quietly here and there, less substance than shadow, their dark eyes beckoning.

At the second knock on his door, Latta turned his head and called curtly, "All right—come in."

Joe Durkin stepped through and closed the door behind him. A burly, large man, it was his job to keep order in the place when it was open for business, and among the Indians at other times, now and then carrying out some special assignment afield. Latta narrowed his eyes when he recognized the faint concern in the man's flinty features.

"What's on your mind, Joe?" he said.

"There was a Injun at the back door just now," Durkin said in his jarring voice. "From the fishing village. That Enos sent him. Said to tell you old Johnson got careless. Luke Prine was tellin' the agent about Jug-Up bein' in the mountains with packs."

There was no change of expression on Latta's face, but he was listening with sudden intentness. "What's that got to do with me?"

"Well, some Injun told Prine you've got a deal with 'em. Guns for gals."

Latta swore softly. In the next breath he had recovered his composure and pulled a cigar from his vest pocket. He bit off the tip of the weed. Now and then the most careful man made a mistake, and it appeared that his turn had come. The chance of Johnson's being caught in Indian country with

14

contraband had always been present, but Latta had supposed it would be some white man who got onto him. Had that happened, Jug-Up would have disclaimed any connection with Lattaville. It would have been accepted that he'd gone into illegal trading on his own hook, to raise money for booze. The chance of an Indian spilling the beans had laid outside Latta's calculations until now.

Latta said sharply, "What'd Wright say about it?"

"He asked Enos, and that's one smart Injun. He laughed at the idea, and Wright called the whole thing hot air. But hadn't I ought to take care of Jug-Up? If Prine or the army fellas grill him, his nerve might crack. That worries me."

"He won't talk about me," Latta said savagely. "I've made it plain what'd happen to Jody, if he did. But I wish it was somebody besides Prine who got his wind up."

A malicious interest flickered in Durkin's eyes. "He carries thousands in gold dust, every time he goes to Crescent. So far he's been rough on the road agents that tackled him, but a smart man could take him. And the dust. Then there'd be no worry and no connection with us."

Latta smiled thinly. He had long felt the challenge of the small fortunes Prine regularly carried on the trail, for nothing fascinated him so much as other people's gold dust and the matter of getting it into his own possession. He lighted the cigar, still smiling, then shook his head. "Maybe, but I'm not sure this is the time."

Durkin turned and laid his hand on the doorknob, then looked back. "I lay 'wake nights wonderin' if that Enos ain't too smart even for us. How do we know he'll really give us warnin'? He don't like white people, and we're white people. Just watchin' his eyes, sometimes, I get buggered."

"He'll warn us," Latta said, easy on that score. It was a gamble, but the odds lay with him that he could be well away from this country, where he had cleaned up, before the Indian pot boiled over.

"So we let it ride?" Durkin said.

"Till I say otherwise."

Latta watched his man's departure with moody eyes. If Durkin failed to get a warning to clear out, it might not be the fault of Enos. Latta was interested in taking only one person out of Curry County ahead of the uprising he knew was coming. Himself.

He glanced at his watch and saw that the afternoon was only half spent. It would be a couple of hours after dark before the miners would knock off work, rustle themselves meals and get around to thinking of the night's pleasures.

That gave him time to walk off some of his restlessness. He got a hat from the closet, donned it, and went down the stairs that descended directly into the saloon. The big room was deserted, but for a moment he stood on the bottom step, looking it over with a curiously impersonal regard. The fixtures and furnishings were all plain and practical, since the men he sought to attract had not taste for better and would only have abused and damaged it. Latta had never felt a pride of ownership as much as an inner exultation that, at long last, he had got hold of a good thing.

The establishment might continue to make money, he thought, except for the changeless fact that the placers had started to taper off, warning of the day when they would play out entirely. Then, even if the Indians tolerated it, there would be nothing here but a population of settlers, making meager livings from a few cows, hogs and chickens, a garden, berry patch and some fruit trees. There would be no money in it for Pete Latta, even if he could stand the boredom of that class of people.

He let himself out the front way and stepped onto the sandy footpath that ran beside the main trail to Sebastopol. From his position the town was lost in the trees, but he could see above and beyond the trees the hills on the north point. Some of the people had built a stockade over there, without knowledge of how much they were going to need it. Idly settling on the route of his stroll, he turned along a lead-off path running down between twin rocks and then dropping through a cleft in the low bluff above the beach. The way was well worn, and as he came over he saw a pair of mining partners working a sluice directly below him. Their cabin stood against the cliff, with the tramped sand about it littered with empty tins and bottles, tools and drift dragged up for fire-wood.

The long sluice bisected the claim and the men, dressed heavily against the raw February air, were steadily feeding it black sand. Water from a small stream, diverted into the sluice, washed the sand down across amalgam plates, leaving the heavier gold on the plates and tumbling the worthless sand on into the surf. Latta relished the scene. All up and down the winter-grayed tidal strip were other trashy domicles and other crude factories of priceless treasure.

He pulled on his cigar, interested in his thoughts. Every sweating shoveler along that beach was a slave of his vices and thus easy to enslave by a man willing to cater to those vices. They saved nothing, all having a simple-minded faith that the black sands were inexhaustible, that out beyond the breakers lay a limitless deposit to be washed in providentially by the storms. Actually, Latta knew, such storms and the frequent high tides only buried existing deposits under plain sand that had to be shoveled aside. He had long ago discovered that everything in the world was limited, that a man had to grab while he could.

One of the miners had noticed him and nodded. Latta nodded stiffly, stepped around their claim and went on to the wet tidal sands. A muggy mist lay over the sea, and when he looked inland he saw that clouds had dissolved the tops of the mountains. He walked with a deliberate looseness, hoping to wear the tension out of his back and shoulders. As he passed claim after claim he nodded or called brief greetings, never stopping to talk. Ten minutes later he rounded the point and saw ahead of him, in the estuary, the wharfs where lay the little merchant marine of the town.

He climbed the slope to a straggling lane that connected the riverfront with Main Street. Houses stood under the trees along the way, homes of family men from whose society he was barred much more to his amusement than regret. He passed the first two places without seeing anyone and then, outside a white picket fence, he halted in quick interest.

A girl stood in the sandy yard beyond, looking up into a fir, calling imploringly, "Here, Plutarch, you naughty kitty —you come down from there!"

Glancing into the half-grown tree, Latta saw a brindle cat, looking down at the girl but motionless as a knot on the limb on which it crouched. He knew the house to be Judge Kelly's. There being so few women on that reach of the coast, the arrival of a new one was a matter of wide interest, especially if she was young, pretty and unmarried. Latta had long ago heard of Carol Dennis, and now for the first time he had the pleasure of seeing, perhaps of helping her.

He dropped the stub of his cigar to the sand and shifted his eyes again to the tall, lovely shape of her back, which was turned to him. He regarded the dark, lustrous hair, in a knot on her neck. He studied the bare arms, held akimbo, and at the exasperated hands planted on the shapely shelves of her hips.

With an angry stamp of her foot, she called, "Plutarch, I've had enough of this!"

Latta spoke then. "He got up there, Miss Dennis. He'll come down when he's ready. He's only being ornery."

She turned with a gasp. Latta had removed his hat and made a slight bow, assured by his grooming and the dark, Latinesque look of face women in San Francisco, and New

Orleans prior to that, had found attractive. They had their effect on Carol Dennis, too. Her annoyance faded. Her dresss was plain but well fitted, and she held herself with the confidence of women who have proved their appeal to men.

"I know he can get down," she said with a toss of the head. "It's a matter of who's boss. You seem to know me. Have we met?"

"Everyone's heard of you, Miss Dennis. I'm Pete Latta. I know your uncle, the judge."

A smile formed on her lips, reflected in the dark eyes that surveyed him. "Oh, yes. The mayor of Lattaville."

"Not exactly." She knew about him and was only interested, a novel experience after being snubbed openly by the distaff side of Gold Beach. And then Latta laughed. The cat, seeing his chance, had dropped from the tree and gone skittering around the house. "Plutarch has given you the slip."

"He's incurable."

She gave Latta a brief smile and turned toward the house.

He held his shoulders a little straighter while he walked on into the town, passed through, and started down the trail to Lattaville.

Before descending for the night's work, Latta took a hot bath in a tub made of staves cut from Port Orford cedar. The soap he used had been brought specially from San Francisco, and he applied it generously, with particular attention to his hands. Then he donned fresh clothing and seated himself to a meal prepared by the one Chinese in Gold Beach, washing down the food with California wine and following it with a cigar of fine Havana.

Afterward he stood by the window, drawing on the cigar, looking down into the dim compound where he had just seen a man move with a girl through one of the many doors. Until his arrangement with Enos, it had been a problem to keep those compartments staffed. Now the Indians did the recruiting. And the price of a rifle, smuggled in from California, was returned tenfold before the woman escaped or grew so troublesome she had to be returned to her people.

Latta walked to the door and opened it only to halt and let his features stiffen. At the same moment a tall man reached the landing beyond, coming up from the now noisy saloon. Latta placed the cigar in his lips and drew on it while Luke Prine stopped before him, dressed in a suit and with a new hat cuffed to the back of his head. Latta would have known he was in trouble without the warning from Enos that afternoon. Prine had never been here before.

Curtly, Prine said, "I want a word with you, Latta."

"Sure. I'm on my way down now."

"I reckon your room'll be better."

Latta shrugged and moved back. Prine followed and shut the door with deliberation. When he refused to sit down, Latta felt uneasiness work in his bone marrow. He waited, his varnished exterior giving little hint of his qualms.

Prine walked to the window at which Latta had stood only a moment before. He took a long look downward before speaking. "What do they get out of it besides beads, booze and abuse, Latta?"

"The girls?" Latta said with a laugh. "What their kind have always wanted. Money."

Prine shook his head. "Fella told me they don't see a grain of dust, that a head woman collects. That makes it look like the money goes into your pocket, Latta."

"I came here to make money. Didn't you?" Latta studied the face before him. Enos' scoffing had not put down Prine's suspicions. He was pursuing the matter relentlessly, and there was danger in his scornful eyes. "Why the sudden interest, Prine? I've been here a long while."

"Ever since the upriver renegades moved into the mountains, our Injuns have been restless and troublesome. Yet they let you have their youngest, best-looking women. To give away their favors to white men. It don't make sense, Latta. Even Injuns pay plenty to get that kind of women." Prine turned back to the window. "Lookin' down there, I get a feelin' they're doin' what Injun women have to do after their men have sold 'em. Or swapped 'em off."

"Swapped? What for?"

"Well, say—guns."

It was in the open finally and Latta let out a slow breath. Prine had turned toward him again, and his eyes were like balls of ice.

"Ever stop to think," Prine resumed, "that what you really swapped for your women is the lives of a lot of white people, including their women and young 'uns? If the boys downstairs knew how you get their pleasure for 'em, they'd string you up."

Shock ran along Latta's bones. He hadn't worried about the military after Wright's easy dismissal of the accusations. But if Prine got the citizenry aroused, things could taken an appalling turn. Latta had difficulty in swallowing, almost as if a rope had already tightened around his neck.

But he managed to say coldly, "I don't know what got you going like this. But what you're saying's as dangerous as it's crazy."

19

Prine shook his head. "Only dangerous. For the whites, the Injuns, and you. You must have your escape figured, but I'm telling you, Latta. If there's an uprisin', and we both come through it, I'll see you hang."

With a look of deep contempt, the expressman walked out.

3 BY NOON Luke had ridden out of the haunts of the coast Rogues and come to the ferry at the Chetco. For some fifteen miles up this stream there now dwelt a related people, named for the river, two of whose villages had once been here at the mouth. On this delayed trip to Crescent City, he came out of the timber cautiously, his saddlebags stuffed with gold dust and outgoing mail filling the leather panniers slung to a pack tree on the horse he led. Three years before an incident had occurred that still made Luke uneasy when he crossed this region to pass on over the California border, which was six miles farther south.

Originally some white men had come over from Smith River, which was on the California side of the line, and taken land claims here. Since the claims were back from the river, the Chetcos occupying the villages on either side at that time had made no objection. Within a few months, however, the mining boom started on the Rogue, bringing a heavy stream of traffic through this country, and crossing the Chetcos became a profitable business for the Indian ferry-owners.

One of the white settlers, remembered only as Miller, had been an aggressive, ambitious man. The trail clung close to the beach, crossing the Chetco at its mouth and making the site a logical place for the town Miller soon aspired to build. So he plotted and declared his town would exist where one of the Chetco villages stood. He built a cabin there for himself and informed the Indians that thereafter his was the exclusive right to ferry the miners. Since the coast Indians had surrendered their few firearms after a treaty arranged a little earlier, the Chetcos were not inclined to dispute him openly.

All went well until late the following winter, and Miller, while failing to realize his hoped-for town, profited greatly from the heavy travel between Crescent City and the mines. But, as he saw it, there was a louse in the bedroll, for the Indians now and then defied his edict and pocketed a ferry toll for themselves. So Miller took steps, bringing several friends over from Smith River to help him.

Luke could still recall the report of the rest of it, which

the then Indian agent had shown him before mailing: "The next morning at daylight the party, consisting of eight or nine well-armed men, attacked the village, and as the Indians came from their lodges, twelve were shot dead. The women and children were allowed to escape. Three Indians remained in the lodges and returned the fire with bows and arrows. Being unable to get a sight of those Indians, the white men ordered two squaws, pets in the family of Miller, to set fire to the lodges. Two Indians were consumed in the conflagration. The third, while raising his head through the flames and smoke for a breath, was shot dead. In the next two days all the lodges at the mouth of the river were burned except two belonging to friends of the women who helped Miller. In all, twenty-three Indians and several squaws were killed. Miller was afterward arrested and placed in the custody of the military at Fort Orford; but upon examination before a justice of the peace was set at large on ground of justification and want of evidence."

Now Luke came down to the river with dread, knowing that if he could not forget the atrocity, the Chetcos were much less apt to. They had moved up the river, and a white replacement for Miller still operated the ferry, now a large raft that had been substituted for the early canoes. Luke felt a knotting of the throat each time he came through until he saw that the new operator had not paid the price of Miller's outrage.

This time he rode down to the ferry slip to see again that all was well. Thurb Perkins' young ones played about the roadside cabin. His thin, shy wife peeked out the door and ducked back when Luke waved to her. Perkins came out of his barn and hurried to the landing.

A rotund man, Perkins said, "Howdy, stranger. I wondered if Kelly's purty niece had got a ring in your nose and the rope tied to a picket pin."

"It hasn't been that long since I was through," Luke returned. "How're the Chetcos behaving?"

"Ain't seen hide nor hair of one all week." The ferry cast off, the leeboard and trolly harnessing the river current to propel it. "Anything new down your way?"

"Well, I don't like the feel of it," Luke confessed. "And if I was you, I'd take my family to Crescent for a while."

"Pshaw, Luke. Me and the missus've been as good to the Injuns as old Miller was mean. We've got no cause to fear 'em."

Riding on, Luke wished that were so, but his confrontation of Pete Latta the night before had convinced him the man was guilty of everything charged. Yet the conclusion rested too much on insight and his own judgment for him to proclaim it publicly. The most he could do was warn of the catastrophe he saw ahead and hope the white settlements would prepare themselves, even if they could get no help from the military. Yet he meant to make one more try for military protection, at least to get word of what he suspected to army headquarters in San Francisco.

He crossed the line and afterward followed the shore of of Pelican Bay to Paradise Valley, where a small settlement had grown up, then passed over Smith River. In late afternoon he reached the first giant redwoods, topped a summit and came down in early evening to Crescent City.

The town lay on a half-moon harbor under a point that sheltered it from the heavy northerlies, a raw, new town bursting with a thousand inhabitants. As yet no pier had been built for the ocean commerce that gave it life, and freight and passengers from the sea came bouncing through the surf in boats and went from boats to horse-carts to be pulled over the shallow tidal flats. The round-about Indians had little in common with those to the north, so that settlement had progressed without undue bloodletting as far as Arcata Bay, which was under the protection of Fort Humboldt. Now, with the unrest in the north, a small detachment of regulars from the fort was encamped at Crescent City.

Luke left his express at the local office of the new Wells-Fargo, took receipts for the gold dust to be turned over to its owners, picked up the mail to go back with him, then stabled his horses. He ate his first meal since breakfast at the Crescent House, where he put up on this end of his run, and in the full darkness made his way to the army camp on the edge of town.

Jones, commanding at Fort Humboldt, was on hand in person, and he received Luke promptly in his tent. A captain, Jones was an old hand on the frontier, and he listened gravely to what Luke had to say about contraband firearms.

"I could be wrong," Luke concluded. "And I hope to hell I am because it's too late to do anything about it. Except, maybe, getting you people to put enough army there to discourage the Injuns from tryin' anything."

"I'll report it," Jones said with a shake of the head, "but I doubt that it'll hurry anything. Like I told you before, General Wool's got his mind set on a spring and summer campaign."

Luke had formed no unreasonable opinion of the difficulties confronting the army. Forts Humboldt and Orford had been established where the settlement was until the mines boomed Gold Beach and created a community that might collapse overnight. In the view of the Pacific Department, in far-off San Francisco, it would be simpler and much easier on a tight military budget for this transient populace to move to the protection of the forts than to take the protection to them.

Grumpily, he said, "I sure hope the Injuns wait till the weather's nice and pleasant."

"I know how you feel, Luke, and I'll try to build a fire under them down there."

Luke was at the livery barn before daylight. His first question to the sleepy stablehand was, "Is she ready?" The man nodded. They walked deeper into the barn, Luke's mouth creasing in a grin. The new horse, a handsome steel gray mare, was with the animals he had brought with him. Luke walked up, spoke gently and patted the mare, then in the yellow lanternlight examined the new sidesaddle he had ordered from San Francisco on a previous trip. He had bought the horse from a rancher down the coast, ordering it well-gentled for it was to be a lady's mount.

"That ought to get you a smile," the hostler said.

"Ain't she a beaut?"

"The lady?"

"I'm thinkin' of this one, at the moment."

The barn hand helped him with the other horses, and Luke was away by daylight. The morning came on clear and warm, the horses were rested, and as he pressed swiftly northward it was easy to forget the worry that nagged him and think about the dance to be held that night at Big Flat. It was to be a barn dance, he had learned, one of the settlers having put up a new barn whose hayloft would be empty until cutting time in the summer. He had asked Carol Dennis, after his supper at Judge Kelly's, and she had been excited, the more so when he warned her the men would outnumber the women ten to one and dance her to a frazzle.

The balmy day drifted on, and over the sea whenever he saw it lay a vast and settling calm. Perkins' joke about the sidesaddle, when Luke ferried the Chetco at midday, built up the illusion of tranquility. At the Pistol River ford, which he reached around two o'clock, he halted to rest the horses. So steadily had he covered the trail, he passed Lattaville and drew in sight of Sebastopol with an hour remaining of daylight.

He had only to ride onto Main Street to detect the festivity inspired throughout Gold Beach by the coming dance, although it was to be held up the river three miles. Sebastopol was mainly an evening and week-end town, periods when the scattered population could assemble. But already the walks were packed with miners drawn early from their diggings to buy shirts and trims from the tinsmith-barber and to start painting their noses to an extent where some of them would never make the gay doings. They noticed Luke, knew a mail had arrived from outside, and trailed him in growing numbers to Gerow's store, the unofficial post office. Luke unloaded and went on at once, with much to do before eight o'clock, when he was to call for Carol.

He would have passed the Johnson cabin without stopping had he not noticed Jody in the yard gathering an armload of firewood. Dropping the horses he led, he rode over to her but did not dismount.

"How come, Jody?" he said. "I thought you'd be all prettied up by now."

"The dance? I'm not going."

"Come now. Must've been a hundred fellas after you."

"Hardly that many." Jody glanced toward the trail. "That's a pretty mare."

Luke nodded, but he found himself embarrassed by the lady's saddle. Everyone else had seemed to know who it and the mare were for, and so would Jody. Some small, peculiar expression had formed on her face. A fine horse and saddle made a costly gift, and he wondered if she considered him extravagant and showy. Awkwardly, he said, "With spring and summer comin', I figured—well—"

"Carol will love it," Jody agreed. "If she can stick on."

Luke stared at her, surprised at what seemed to be scorn of Carol's ladylike habits. Jody could split wood, milk a cow, row a boat, spade a garden, and when she rode a horse she went aboard like a man. Coming up from Crescent City, when she first arrived, Carol had been obliged to ride that way, there being no sidesaddle in the country, but it had distressed her. She had discouraged his efforts to take her riding, since, and he had come up with this idea, and he didn't like having it made to look ridiculous.

"Why, she's a fine rider," he said. "But all dressed up for goin' to a dance, a lady can't—" He broke off, aghast at himself. Carol's frocks and gowns and doodads were the talk of the beach, and the doubted that Jody even had a best dress. Awkwardly, he said, "But I got to get crackin'. Sorry you won't be there, Jody. Figured on you and me doin' a little stompin' together." She glanced at him quickly, but the

24

truculence didn't leave her eyes. He touched his hatbrim and left.

When he rode back by her cabin a little before eight o'clock, all he could see was a lighted window. He had eaten, shaved, taken a bath in the creek and put on his best clothes. He had rubbed the steel mare with a gunnysack and now led it alone. He entered town, crossed the end of Main and went on down the wharf road to the Kelly house.

Carol was nowhere near ready, and Luke had to sit in the parlor and talk with the judge for fifteen minutes before she descended the stairs and nearly stopped his breath. She wore a full-skirted dress that hid her feet, and there were lacings in the upper part that brought out some mighty nice details of her figure. Her dark hair was piled high on her head, and there were gimcracks in her tiny ears, and her dark eyes shone.

"Lord Almighty," Luke gasped.

"Like it?" Carol made a complete, happy turn in front of him.

Mrs. Kelly had followed Carol down the stairs. She carried a wrap that she handed to Luke, and he got it through his dazed head that he was to help Carol into it. He did so, giddy from the delightful scent that struck his nostrils. The judge, pulling on a cigar, had a twinkle in his eyes. He said, "Mind you come straight home afterward," and Luke blushed and Carol laughed. Then Luke ushered her out into a night suddenly soft and warm and wonderful.

They were nearly to the waiting horses when Carol stopped in her tracks. "A sidesaddle! Luke! Where did you ever find it?"

He grinned happily. "Fresh out of 'Frisco, and the fella gentled the mare specially for a lady, and it's all yours, Carol."

"To keep? Oh—Luke!"

The rest happened so fast his senses reeled. She turned and threw her arms around his neck, raising tiptoe, while his heart slammed his ribs. She kissed him smack on the mouth with lips sweet as clover honey, and then had slipped away before he could recover his wits and cooperate.

He swung her up, adjusted the stirrup, made sure her other knee was hooked securely, then they rode up the river together.

4   So MUCH MOISTURE had seeped through the long crack in the mirror, which hung on the log wall by the door, that Jody had to stand just to see herself at all. Not that the costliest of mirrors could have made her happier with her reflection. About her shoulders was the shawl that was one of the few things remaining of her dead mother's, and she folded it higher on her neck to see if that helped any. Even if it had—which it did not—she snorted as she looked down at the faded calico of her dress and her heavy shoes. She owned nothing better.

No different, she thought, from what nearly all the women would wear, but how clumsily those clogs would bang compared to the dainty slippers of Carol Dennis. Whatever had got into her, the morning she gave Luke pie and coffee, to make her blurt that out about the dance in some wild, senseless hope that he would ask her, when he'd had eyes for no one but Carol since she came to the country. Jody was glad that he hadn't asked her, that he had no idea that she'd had eyes for no other man since he came to Gold Beach.

She walked away from the mirror and crossed to the fireplace, still wearing the shawl because she liked the soft feel of wool between her hairline and the neck of her dress. The log fire roared on its dried-mud stage, and this was one of the rare times when she need not consider it merely as a means of converting dough to bread-stuffs. She looked dreamily into the flames, imagining the couples—whirling, backing, filling and swaying to the music and the caller's chants.

She turned her head, delayed in her notice of a rap on the door. She frowned, wondering what man could have stayed away from the dance to be wanting a loaf of bread at this hour. She was not a shy one, for she dealt with many men, but she didn't like it when they came at night, with her father gone as now. But she went across to the door and opened it.

Pete Latta stood there, looking at her, smiling. There was an insolence behind his expression that angered her.

"Evening, Jody," he said, pulling off his hat and making an exaggerated bow. "Jug-Up home?"

"He's not, and don't you come smilin' around me, Pete Latta. You've been sellin' him booze again."

"He did some work for me, Jody, and that's how he wanted his wages."

"I've asked and asked you—"

Latta laughed, stepped in and shut the door behind him, so

deliberately that her anger turned back into worry. He tossed his hat on a chair, walked on over to the fire, meanwhile pulling a cigar from his vest and sticking it in his lips. He was eying her with a deliberate interest that made her flush. She had no illusions about being pretty but knew her hard slim body appealed to men, that according to their natures they decently or indecently wanted her. Latta's interest was of the latter sort, as he had more than once made plain.

"He's past curing, Jody," Latta said. "You'd ought to give up on that. Where is he?"

"Since he don't have to cadge drinks right now, thanks to you, he's likely over with some cronies on Crawdad Bar." Then, suspiciously, "What do you want of him?"

"Just to ask him something." Latta looked at her shrewdly. "Know if he's talked to Luke Prine the last few days?"

"Luke was here the other morning, but Pa was too far gone to talk to anybody."

Something eased in Latta. He smiled and finally lighted his cigar. "Why aren't you at the dance?"

"Why aren't you?"

He laughed. "The same reason you aren't. We're outcasts, Jody. You the daughter of the town drunk. Me a whore-monger. We ought to comfort one another."

He didn't shock her. She knew her station in Gold Beach, and she knew about the Indian women at Lattaville. But she said tartly, "Mind your tongue, Pete Latta."

"When're you going to get enough of it, Jody?"

"I've had more than enough—"

"I don't mean my tongue. When are you going to leave Jug-Up to pickle in his own brine and start leading your own life? I'm going to 'Frisco pretty soon. I would help you get a start down there."

"Doing what?"

He drew on the cigar. "Lots of ways for smart women, specially when they're built like you are, to make money. Lots of it. Money, clothes, jewels—everything you don't have now. How about coming with me? I'm not such bad company."

"No thanks."

Latta picked up his hat. "You might wish you had."

She was relieved when he left. A time or two, when he had been drinking, he had been on the verge of getting recklessly rough with her. She dropped the bar across the door so it couldn't be opened from outdoors and went back to the fire, the smell of Latta's cigar heavy on the air. She wondered why he thought she would be sorry for refusing to go away with him, when she had no illusions about the kind of life he had in mind. She walked to the east window and stared out into the heavy darkness. Big Flat was too far away for her to see the lights in the new barn where they were having the dance. Latta had told her once she had the makings of a striking woman, that she had something rarer than prettiness. She wondered how true this was and why she had never discovered the secret of it for herself.

Her usual bedtime had come and passed, and there was no use sitting up mooning because she was restless and unhappy, this night. She glanced at the door, knowing she should leave it unfastened so her father could get in, in case he was able to make it home at all. But the uneasiness Latta had aroused still haunted her, and she left the bar in place. Her father could pound on the door if he wanted in.

It seemed to her that she had scarcely shut her eyes when this happened, but it must have been two or three hours later. She heard a hammering, then her father's ragged voice shouting, "Jody! Open up! For God's sake—Jody!"

"Just a minute, Pa."

She got sleepily from her bed in the lean-to while he kept pounding and calling in that imploring voice. By the time she crossed to the door the fact had seeped through her drowsy senses that something was very wrong. She slid back the bar hurriedly, and the door swung inward. Her father stumbled into the room, sagged over and gasped in loud, tearing noises.

"Not again," she said in mechanical disgust.

And then she saw it. A feather-tipped shaft stuck grotesquely out from her father's back, left of the spine and just under the ribs. She realized in horror that it had gone deep. Her father reeled around, gasping, his weak, whiskery face wizened with pain and terror.

"My pistol—Jody, my God—we gotta—"

"Pa, what is it?"

"Injuns—they're all over—"

He was staggering around the room now, hunting the old pistol he carried when he was off on a trip. The way he bumped into things, she saw he was half-blinded. Jody ran to the window and looked out and saw blazing light at the bar up the river where two miner friends of his lived. Their cabin was on fire, blazing high, not half a mile away. It began to make sense then, the uprising everybody predicted but hoped would never happen. Fright dug claws into her own throat. She found the pistol but held on to it since he was in no shape to handle it. She slammed shut the door.

"No," her father croaked at her. "They'll be here in a minute—burn us alive if they can't get in—we gotta hide—!"

That made sense to Jody, too. She flew into the bedroom and grabbed her clothes and shoes, although she dared not take time to dress. Her father had dropped onto a chair and sat dragging in painful breaths, the arrow sticking out of his back.

"Go," he groaned. "I—can't. I'm—tuckered out—"

"No. Come on."

She helped him to his feet and all but carried him into the strangely silent night. From there she saw a second fire, farther up the river than the bar. But there was no sound of shooting. If the Indians had truly risen up, which she did not doubt, they were doing it stealthily so as not to spread a warning. She staggered off into the darkness with her father's lurching weight upon her.

She hadn't thought about where to hide, but some memory of people submerging themselves in water until danger passed must have stirred in her mind, for she found herself crossing the trail and working down toward the river. Her father's breath was a rushing noise, and he was hardly able to put one foot ahead of the other to keep from falling while she dragged him along. Then they reached the river brush, and she pulled him into it and finally let him sag down.

"You're a good swimmer, Jody," he gasped. "Mebbe—you could make it—over. It's—your best—chance—"

"I'm not going to leave you, Pa. What happened?" She began to dress.

"Just settin' there," he mumbled presently. "Three of us. Havin' a little drink. And they busted in—a dozen—fightin' all over the place. Don't know how I got out. Then one whanged—an arrow—and—" He could say no more.

She kept dressing, watching him through the darkness, slowly understanding the implication of what he had managed to reveal. He could have found hiding places as good as this much closer, and he had the arrow in him, but he had driven himself home to warn her. The boozy ugliness fell away, and she saw him again as the man he had been before her mother died, the woman he had loved too much, whose leaving he could not endure. A lump ached in her throat and she dropped to her knees beside him.

"We'll make it, Pa," she whispered. "It's all right."

"Not me, Jody—and—we gotta think. You could—swim the —river, mebbe—"

"I'm not gonna—" She knew why she had never been able to abandon him.

"Hush."

Jody heard the sound, too, hardly audible above the babble of the river. She crept to the edge of the brush, the pistol fisted, and looked along the trail toward the burning cabins and the Indian village far beyond. She saw nothing until she looked across the trail and up toward their own cabin. She gasped. Nearly naked bodies glinted up there in the moonlight. They had kept off the trail, slipping through the grass and brush. They had found the door unlocked and gone in but had found nobody there to murder. They had looked about for loot, then scattered the fire. She could see the flames leaping up inside. Then she glanced toward Sebastopol and nearly cried out.

The town had been all but emptied by the dance at Big Flat, and those who remained had long since gone to their beds. The Indians had entered the town in the same stealthy way, and on the edge of it there were burning buildings. She looked back to see that the figures about the Johnson cabin had vanished, drawn toward the town. She wanted to cry a warning to the people there, to rush along the trail in shouting urgency. She knew it would be a futile folly, that she could do nothing to help them.

She crept back to her father, who lay on his side and was mumbling. When she bent closer to listen, she heard, "Forgive me—God—Jody—"

"Pa, it's all right."

"No—I'm guilty—I took 'em guns—for Latta—"

He gasped, wrenched, then was motionless. In a moment she realized that he was dead.

Her first reaction was one of terrible loneliness, and she stood hidden in the river growth, incapable of thinking what to do now. The idea of trying to swim the river to the uninhabited north shore frightened her as much as the vague but awful peril filtering through the night on this side. The flames of the burning town leaped above the trees now, but she knew that intervening buttes and timber would keep them from being seen at Big Flat. The flat might itself be under attack, although nearly all the young and able had gathered there and many of them were in the habit of carrying firearms. The thought of this large assembly drew her, yet the three intervening miles of unfathomable darkness held her still.

And then the import of her father's confession began to come through. She had never had more than a vague understanding of what he did for Latta when he was away. Her main concern had been over the fact that he would drink up what he had earned, lying sodden and disgusting in the cabin until she could hardly bear it. Now, slowly and inalterably, she understood that, in exchange for the alcohol he so unremittingly craved, he had helped to arm the Indians. Those fierce, spreading flames and the people dead, dying and yet to die, were part of the price for his bouts of insensible escape. The shame of that was on her now, greater than her shame of the drunkenness and poverty. There was nothing left for her to fear because there was nothing left for her to save.

Flames licked through the roof of the Johnson cabin, and even as she pondered she watched the destruction of the home she had tried to make there for her father and herself. That gave her no feeling, for walls and roofs could be raised anew. Pots, pans, dishes, clothing, furniture—all the accessories of living could be accumulated again. Life was what mattered, but without pride it was intolerable.

And yet . . .

The life that was in her leaped even more strongly when the cabin roof caved in. It leaped higher when, a moment afterward, something exploded in the town to shower sound and embers on the growing scene of desolation. She lived, and while she lived she hoped, and that was stronger than shame and fear and emptiness. She lived this once and never again, and a moment later that knowledge made her press deeper into hiding in renewed panic. A party of Indians came trotting down the trail from the dying town, stripped for war, their painted faces hideous in the glow of the fires. She could hear the thud of their moccasins as they went by on the trail, showing themselves boldly, now that they completely controlled the area.

She bent over her father for a last long look then, clutching the pistol, she cut across the trail, swung around the burning cabin and headed for the timbered ridge south of it. Nothing intervened except the darkness and its pitfalls, but she knew the area intimately and moved swiftly. Ten minutes later she was on the ridgeline, with a wider view of what was happening. To the west Lattaville burned with the same intensity as Sebastopol, and she could see the burning cabins of miners all along the beach. But inland the look was less frightening.

Elephant Rock lay like a drowned monster off the mouth of the creek at the east foot of the ridge on which she stood. Above it the cabin from which her father had fled to warn her was a tumbled bed of burning ruins. The nearly burned buildings on above that would be at the ferry. Above them, and back from the river, there was nothing to indicate trouble so far. If she stayed this far south of the Rogue and could get through without a trail to follow, she might reach the barn dance at Big Flat in time.

5   IT HAD GROWN so hot in the hayloft, all but the determined and inexhaustible had found other places to enjoy themselves. Some were on the ground floor of the barn, sitting around trying to talk against the ceiling-jarring racket above. Even more were in the yard, where a score of jugs had been hidden in the grass. Another group had repaired to the settler's cabin, where a collation prepared by the settler women had been spread on planks laid across sawhorses.

George Murphy was calling the dance, and he had a voice like a bugle to which the flying feet made drums. "Balance one—balance all eight—swinging on the corner—like swinging on a gate—"

Luke had come down from the loft and stood outside the barn door with his hands shoved into his hip pockets and a frown on his features. They had got this quadrille going, and once again his partner of the evening had been taken from him. She had become community property almost on arrival, his scowls cancelled by her friendly smiles. But she was having a wonderful time after a long, dull winter, and he had tried to be good humored about it.

"Bird hop out—crow hop in—seven hands up and round again—"

Hy Galtry, who ran a packstring for one of the town merchants, came out the door and began to stuff his pipe. He said cheerfully, "If Alf's new barn hadn't got done settlin', it sure has now."

"They're givin' it a poundin'," Luke agreed.

Galtry sighed. "Wish I was that young again. They'll keep doin' it till daylight."

Luke knew that was true, and it had been two o'clock the last time he looked at his watch. He'd had a schottische and Virginia reel with Carol in the past hour, no more. He knew he wouldn't have much more of her until they started home, riding along together through the night. He looked forward to it and wondered how much longer she could last.

Galtry said, "How about a cup of coffee?"

"Guess I'd better get back to the hoedown."

The packer strolled away toward the cabin. Luke was about to turn back through the barn door when his glance fell on something off to the west, a figure dimly seen against the brush. The shape moved, and his gaze sharpened. That was a woman. She came forward in a staggering way, and Luke went striding toward her, taking her for somebody from the dance until he drew closer. She was Jody Johnson.

Others had seen her, too, read the significance of it, and were also moving toward her. But Jody saw only Luke and started running to meet him.

"Jody! What is it?"

She put her face against his chest and gave way to wrenching sobs. He steadied her, his hands on the back of her shoulders, feeling her trembling. She had come cross-country, steering clear of the river trail, and the worries he had put out of his mind for the dance were realities even before she explained.

"Jody, was it Injuns?"

She nodded. "They killed Pa—everybody. They've burned up everything. There's nothin'—nothin' left down there."

"Oh, my God."

The voice was behind Luke, and for a moment it was the only sound nearer than the racket from the barn. The silence spread as people moved, quieting the cabin and then the barn and hayloft. Jody had come a long way through a night ridden with terror, but she lost control of herself only for a moment. Then she told the throng that was soon gathered about her what she had been through. It created shock more than panic. Many of the listeners had left relatives and friends down the river. Nearly all of them had left property in some form. Yet that was not the immediate concern. The Indians had dug up the hatchet and tasted blood, and all hell couldn't hold them now.

The women took Jody to the cabin, tried to get her to eat a bite, to drink some hot coffee. Many of them had shunned her until then, but now forgot their doubts in her loss, their common danger and her own courage. The men stayed outdoors, rifles and pistols dicarded for the dance reclaimed. They, and most of all Luke, wondered why they had played so blindly into the Indians' hands when the signs of disaffection now seemed so clear. They had invited attack on the lower river by leaving it so helpless, and they had been given a reprieve so far only because they were in large number.

"Well, boys," Hy Galtry said calmly, "it's a question as to our best move. From what Jody says, it's too late to help anybody down below. If they ain't all dead, they're hidin', and the Injuns seem to have come back up the river. They're leery of us so far, likely thinkin' we've got more shootin' irons than we have. So we best be away from here by daylight, when they can get a look at us. That ain't far off."

"Where'll we go?" somebody said.

"If we can make it to the stockade, we might hold out till we can get help."

"Help?" somebody said and laughed. "Where from?"

Luke agreed both with Galtry's suggestion and the other man's pessimism. This would be a hard place to defend, even if they had been better prepared. Yet the stockade that had been built for this very emergency was four or five miles from there, across the river and a mile and a half up the beach from Sebastopol. And his heart sank when he thought of the twenty-six regulars at Fort Orford, the twenty-five at Cresent City, and General Wool's sluggish plans for a campaign after the weather grew better.

An argument broke out then. Some of them held that the best plan was to make it down the river to the two schooners tied up at the wharf, in hopes that they had not been burned with the town. But others pointed out that the little vessels were not ready for sea, even if the season was such that they could safely put out across the bar. Without provisions, they couldn't even be anchored in midstream and used as fortresses. The stockade itself might have been put to the torch, but it was soon agreed that it was the best hope. George Murphy would try to take them to it, after the way had been scouted. Since they were the most experienced trailsmen, Galtry and Luke would try to get help from outside.

"You try for Fort Orford," Galtry said quietly to Luke. "I ain't been up that way much, and I go to Cresent all the time."

Luke nodded and found Carol, dreading it since there wasn't much chance that her aunt and uncle had come through the massacre alive. Someone had helped her down from the hayloft, and she was in the cabin, her pretty face shocked slack, the skin white as a bleached clamshell. He apologized for having to leave her, assured her that she would be in good hands, but she hardly heard him.

Within ten minutes, Luke left with Galtry and four others to scout the river to its mouth. If the way seemed open to the main group, the four others would return to it, while he and the packer went on. They rode north toward the river, approaching it cautiously but informed by the lack of barking dogs that the fishing village had been deserted. The cabin of the Indian agent, a short distance below the village, was a bed of red coals at which they stopped only long enough to see a charred human skeleton where a bunk must have been.

"Ben Wright," Galtry muttered.

The sight was gruesome, but Luke couldn't help thinking of the Modoc village Wright had annihilated to become Yreka's hero and an Indian savant and fighter of wide repute. For all its savagery, tonight's work had been provoked, and quite probably it had originated with the very Enos who had enjoyed Wright's complete trust.

The ferry house, farther down, had been destroyed, its occupants slain, but the scow and guyline had been left intact by the Indians in their hurry. Luke and two others crossed, while Galtry and the other two continued on down the south side. Even on the north bank the smell of smoke grew stronger, then the lingering glow of the burned town grew visible on the other side.

A little later Luke and his companions reined in to stare across at a staggering sight, even though the fire had passed its climax. Great heaps of coals remained from the conflagration, with standing timbers and tree snags that glowed in the smoky night. The little ships had been spared, and their position let Luke fix the location of Judge Kelly's house. It was gone with the rest. He could not escape Jody's belief that few, if any, had been left alive over there. It had all happened too quietly and too fast.

The Port Orford trail turned north from there, edging the beach, and presently burned cabins of miners made it all too clear that a raiding party had been on this side of the river, too. But the hostiles had not gone as far up as the stockade, whose shape presently lifted out of the night. This stood on an open prairie above the beach, the site chosen because it lacked cover for the use of an attacking force. There were two log structures to provide shelter, and about these a high earth embankment had been thrown up. Some of the water of a stream that flowed through the stockade had been diverted into the ditch from which the dirt had come. This created a moat crossed by a bridge that could be drawn up. It was a work of considerable effort by men whose foresight was now proved.

Yet Luke's relief was tempered, for the stockade was empty, ending his hope that survivors from the town and beach would be found here. He took leave of his companions there and rode on, having nearly thirty miles to cover to reach the army fort, with day threatening to break at any moment.

But dawn showed that he was out of the area so far covered by the raiders, and he rode on through a morning of gray fog that deepened the gloom of the coast. Later he grew puzzled as to why a band of friendly Indians who dwelt on Euchre Creek and around Three Sisters Rocks had vanished. Somehow they had got word of the uprising in advance. While Luke doubted that they had gone to join the hostiles, their fading showed how thoroughly the Indians of the area had been posted on coming events. Enos, he thought. The Indian who always knew what the whites were doing and went everywhere among his red brothers. A traitor, and yet a less despicable one than Pete Latta.

In late forenoon Luke reached Port Orford, a larger, more substantial town than Sebastopol had been, serving a wholly agricultural settlement. Captain Tichenor had founded it at the start of the Gold Rush, hoping to make it a seaport for the mining camps springing up in the interior. But no way for a good road had been found through the mountains, and the port dwindled, serving only the settlers who came in under the protection of the fort the army established on the edge of town.

Luke rode onto the sandy street to observe a high-keyed bustle and excitement. Unusual numbers were on hand, and there was a steady traffic between the town and the army post on The Heads, a short distance to the northwest. He reined in at a group of homespun settlers.

"You folks had Injun trouble?" he asked.

A man studied him and said thoughtfully, "Ain't you Prine, from Gold Beach? Then you know more'n we do. Some Euchre Injuns come in yesterday and asked the fort for protection. Said the Rogues'd wiped out you folks."

"They were only ahead of schedule."

Luke told them what had brought him, then rode on to see spread around the fort the camps of a great many Indians. And not only Indians. Nearly as many white people had reached the post, with more on the way, although this area was well removed from the scene of hostilities. He was known by the army garrison and had no trouble gaining admittance to the office of the commanding officer, Major Reynolds, who regarded him sourly.

"Might as well save your breath," Reynolds snapped. "I can't do a thing that I couldn't the last time you were here. You saw the homesteaders and Indians out there. They didn't expect us to garrison every damned claim and peaceful village in the country. When trouble threatened, they came here. And that's what you people should've done and will still have to do if I'm to help you with the feeble resources at my disposal."

Luke towered over the officer's desk. "By God, Major. What we should've done and what you should've done is water over the dam. It's happened. There's maybe fifty dead at Gold Beach and twice that number trying to make it even to our stockade, a mile and a half above town. If they get there, they can hold out only as long as the grub and ammunition they can scare up on short notice will last. If they don't get help before it's gone, there'll be a hundred and fifty dead, a lot of 'em women and children, and don't tell me the U. S. Army's helpless to prevent it."

"What do you expect me to do with twenty-six troops and two hundred refugees who've come here for protection?"

"Make up a supply train, and I'll ram it through. If you haven't got the stuff, you have the authority to requisition it from the town. I haven't, or I'd do it myself."

Reynolds pondered for a long moment, then shook his head. "That's impossible. My responsibility is to the people in my military district, which is Port Orford and vicinity. If this thing spreads, we could be under the seige ourselves and need what we have on hand and more. I'm sorry, but I didn't write the damned book. I just have to do what it says."

Luke knew it was hopeless, that he would have done better had he stayed at Gold Beach and helped out there. The merchants of the town would grant him no credit for goods they might need desperately themselves and which he well might lose long before he reached Gold Beach. No one would furnish the pack animals, and probably no one would volunteer to help him in the effort to get a train through country now overrun by hostile Indians. He could only hope that Hy Galtry had more success in Cresent City, if he made it through. Without another word to the brevet major, Luke turned on his heel and strode out to his horse. He didn't even stop in the alarmed town, although he hadn't eaten since the evening before.

Nightfall found him near Three Sisters Rocks, and he stopped there for an hour to graze and rest his horse. Personally he was past feeling fatigue or hunger or anything except the drive that carried him. An oceanic wind sprang up when he rode on, holding the threat of rain. Then, in about an hour, he dropped down toward the Euchre Creek ford, only to rein in abruptly. A bonfire burned down there, partly screened by the trees. His tired senses snapped into focus, for no refugee trying to make Port Orford would stop and light a fire. He pulled his rifle from the saddle boot and sat holding it for another moment. Then he let the horse move slowly on.

The shot that rang out was that of another rifle, and it came from his right, toward the beach. That confirmed his already strong suspicion that those were Indians at the fire. With his presence discovered, noise was of no moment, and he whipped the horse off the trail, to the left, while another rifle shot split the night. He heard the hum of this bullet, then reached the cover of the brush and thinly spaced trees. His assailant seemed to be afoot, for Luke was well away when a moment later a shot was fired haphazardly into the night behind him.

He kept riding, on the creek now and moving upstream. It was some time before he found a place to ford and crossed over. Another hour or two would bring him to the stockade, but his anxiety only deepened. He understood more fully now why the peaceful Euchres had left the vicinity. The hostiles had taken over here to cut communications with Port Orford and the army post. Undoubtedly they had likewise cut the trail to Cresent City, probably in the easily held position at the Chetco ferry. That cast doubt on Hy Galtry's ability to get through.

As he pressed on, Luke began to discern the plan in what was happening. The hostiles were attempting to seize a fifty-mile corridor running from their mountain stronghold to the open sea, which they meant to rid of its remaining white occupants. Their eastern bulwark had been held successfully against a large military force in the interior. This corridor on their rear would give them living space and provender, for the Rogue teemed with salmon and the lowland valleys with fruits, nuts, berries and small game. If successful, they might hold out indefinitely against outside enemies, and the doom of those caught inside was sealed.

6   PETE LATTA had been in a pleasant frame of mind before the massacre. The dance at Big Flat had played hob with his patronage, with only a handful of dedicated drinkers and gamblers preferring his establishment to the dance. These single-minded addicts made company little to his taste, so he had left the saloon in the care of Joe Durkin and sallied forth for another of his aimless walks.

Latta's own thoughts had been drawn strongly to the dance, for he knew that Carol Dennis would attend, and he had even toyed with the idea of gracing it with his own presence. For his part, he scorned the hostility he knew he would encounter. His decision to stay away had rested on the effect so widespread an antagonism might have on the Dennis girl if she saw it too clearly demonstrated. She had been open-minded in her attitude toward him the day he stopped to help her rescue her treed cat. He wouldn't mind knowing her better, for ladies of exquisite breeding had always attracted him, not only because he appreciated the cultivated but because, when women of that class responded to him, his sense of worth was enhanced. He knew that if he baited the settler women too callously, they could turn Carol completely against him with their lurid talk.

Leaving his establishment, Latta had gained the deserted streets of Sebastopol before he thought of Jug-Up Johnson and decided that this was an opportunity to see the man and determine whether he had been grilled by Luke Prine and how much the addle-witted Jug-Up might have let slip to Prine. So Latta had turned up the river trail toward the tacky Johnson cabin, finishing a cigar as he moved along. What Jody told him about Prine's being at her cabin, and about his being baffled by her father's state of sodden drunkenness, had convinced Latta that the expressman was going entirely on what the bigmouthed Indian in the mountains had told him, with no other evidence of the illegal sale of guns.

By the time Latta left the Johnson cabin he had dismissed the matter, for by then his thoughts were centered on Jody. She interested him in a way directly opposite to his interest in Carol Dennis. As close to a child of nature as a woman could get, Jody was nonetheless a much handsomer woman than she had ever realized. She was a woman more potentially passionate than her aloofness indicated, and a woman far more chaste than her position warranted. These ironies intrigued Latta for, according to the rules as he knew them, she should have been easy pickings for the first personable man to come along. The difference between her and Carol, he reflected as he strolled through the night, was that Carol would yield to a man from courtship, Jody from brute conquest. Constituted as he was, a mixture of gentleman and ruffian, he could not help responding to both challenges.

Letta found that he had regained the benighted streets of the deserted town, and he was not in a mood to return at once to Lattaville. For a moment he paused on a corner of Main Street, glancing along the lampless windows of the buildings. There were times, and this was one, when he felt a strong wish to mingle with his fellow men, as well as the women. None of the business places was open. Even the respectable saloonkeepers, he thought, were welcome at the dance. Along the street that ran to the wharf he saw light in a couple of houses, one Judge Kelly's. Latta smiled thinly. If he went down there and rapped on the judge's door, he wouldn't even be asked to come inside. He paid fifty cents for his Havanas, while Kelly was happy with a cheap cigar, yet the lawyer would snub him.

Deciding to go home by way of the beach, Latta passed along the main street and followed a twisting path down through the wind-bent trees onto the sand. There he seated himself on a drift log, for the sea was calm, stretching away into mystery under the stars. He relighted his cigar, which had gone out in his absorption, and his residual restlessness gave way to a surprising sense of peace. Maybe, he thought, because the sea was so quiet, its soft sibilance shattered only when, somewhere, water crashed on water. The tide was almost at ebb.

This wild and lonely reach of seacoast had enough in common tonight to remind him of Monterey. He had been born there, the offspring of a *paisano* and a *gringo* sailor off a trading schooner in port. He had known poverty of the most grueling kind, and stigma from being the bastard get of his mother's loose conduct. Had her dalliance been with a *caballero*, Latta thought, his illegitimacy would not have made him unacceptable. But she had laid with an unlettered *gringo* deckhand with a dirty, tarred pigtail hanging on his neck.

He owned it to a kindly mission padre that he had not remained unlettered, and from the mission people he had learned good manners and proper language, taking pride in these accomplishments because he knew he was an outcast. By the time of the American conquest, he had been old enough to shake California's dust from his heels and go to New Orleans, where he had learned cards and how to surivive in spite of his lowly origin. Then he came back to California with the Gold Rush, but he hadn't found his main chance until he moved north to Gold Beach, which proved to be his bonanza.

Latta sat there for he knew not how long, his thoughts agreeable, his mood of tranquillity so rare. Then something made him twist on the log and glance back toward the town. Even as he turned his head he heard an astonishing sound, like the scream of a woman. The hair on the back of his neck seemed to come erect, and he shoved to his feet the better to look at the town's timbered obscurity. Even then he began to guess what it was.

He swung, deeply troubled, and started swiftly toward

Lattaville. He had covered but half the distance when he saw flames shoot up down there.

He froze in his tracks, his fear momentarily put down by an enormous anger. Enos. The uprising had come without the warning that had been part of the bargain. When Latta turned, he saw flames reach higher than the trees of Sebastopol, as well. He stood there, helplessly raging at the treachery of the Indian, at the stupidity that had let him come away from his place without his gun.

His anger changed to dismay, and he swung toward his own burning buildings, choking out, "No—!" He broke into an open run along the beach then, careless of the Indians who would be lurking everywhere about. His treasure, all the gold dust he had accumulated, was buried under the floor of a storeroom up there. He was a soft man and was soon winded, and in a moment he was forced to slow down. Despair helped drain away his strength, for by then flames shot high above the roof of his main building, the structures in his compound, and even the miners' shacks in the vicinity. He halted finally, his chest heaving, and looked back to see that Sebastopol had become an inferno of burning buildings and timber.

His lungs heaved in air that now reeked of smoke, and he tried to reassert the supremacy of his cool, gambler's mind over his panicked nerves. Even to save his life, he would not flee the country without the fortune that had been his sole purpose in living here, despised and shunned, for so long. The gold could not be destroyed. The ruins of his doomed establishment would cool enough for him to retrieve it. His immediate problem was only how to survive until that could be done. The realization calmed him down.

He thought of the dance at Big Flat. If there were to be many survivors of this bloody rampage, they would be there where a hundred or so men had gathered. From the stealthy way it was happening, Latta decided that the dancers had been passed by and left until the town that sustained them had been destroyed. Then, without provisions and the stores' stocks of ammunition, the rest would be easy prey.

Latta had never expected to be here during this phase, and he felt himself shudder.

He moved into the brush back of the beach and there hid himself, beginning to shake. He could not hope to reach Big Flat with the country between alive with Indians skulking the night in the loosened lust for blood. He waited, swayed between fits of reckless anger at Enos and waves of sick fear. Now he could hear staccato chains of explosions resulting

41

from burning ammunition stocks, and once a jarring *whoom* meant that gun powder had exploded. Numbly he watched the destruction of Lattaville and the burial of his hard-won fortune under fiery mounds of coals. He wondered, without concern, what had become of the dozen or so men who had been there, including Joe Durkin. Latta had been near enough to hear shooting, but he did not remember any. No, the contraband guns had not come into play. Clubs, knives and stealthy surprise had done the bloody work so far. He wondered if there was anybody besides himself left alive down here.

He knew another moment of panic when he realized, eventually, that someone was coming along the trial beyond the brush where he was hidden. He nearly stopped breathing, the sickness churning in his stomach and burning his throat. When it dawned on him that the oncomers were noisier than Indians would be, he moved to the trail edge of the brush. In a moment he nearly shouted. The party coming toward him from the direction of Lattaville was composed of four white men. One was Durkin and the others miners who had been in a card game earlier. To Latta's regret, he saw that none of them was armed.

He stepped out to meet them, nearly causing them to bolt for the brush themselves. Then, recognizing him, they came on up.

"I told yuh!" Durkin said with a convulsive blurt. "God-damn it, Mr. Latta, I told you that sneakin'—!"

Horrified by the thought that Durkin was about to blab out his own resentment of Enos' treachery, Latta interrupted, "Couldn't you get hold of a gun?"

A miner said bitterly, "By God, Latta, we're lucky we got away with our lives. Them squaws of your'n let a bunch of bucks into the place. The first we knew they were swarmin' all over us. Us four was by the door, so we got out, but—" He shuddered. "We hid in the brush till they'd gone."

"Which way did they head?" Latta asked.

"They took the squaws from the cribs, set everything on fire, and then went hell a-hikin' toward town."

"Where are you planning to go?"

"Well, that stockade they built up the beach seems the best to us, if we can make it across the river. Elvek here thinks he knows where there's a rowboat we can use, if the Injuns ain't took it or cut it loose."

That seemed a more hopeful move to Latta, as long as he would have company, than trying to work eastward through Indian country in an attempt to find sanctuary at Big Flat.

He fell in, and the party went on. Closer to the ruined town, they could see that not a structure had been spared the torch of the Indians' work of vengeance. The business buildings had all but caved in, and off among the burned and burning trees there was not a house or cabin that was not in flames or already a bed of red ruins. Most of the dwellings had been emptied by the dance, but a few had been occupied when the raiders struck. If there were survivors among these, nothing indicated what they had done with themselves.

Latta's party slanted off to the beach to make its way around the conflagration. By the time they turned up the river at its estuary, the smoke was chokingly thick and blinding. They stumbled through the hot, fouled air until they were above the town, and then the smoke was thinner. But when they came to the cove above town where Elvek had thought they might find a boat, there was no boat to be seen. Since the Indians seemed to have left this vicinity, too, it seemed as good a place to wait as any until they could think of some other way to get over the river. Latta would have given much for just one of the guns in which he had trafficked so carelessly with the Indians.

It lacked an hour of daybreak when Hy Galtry came down the river from Big Flat with a party of heavily armed, shocked and very angry men. The moment the lurkers were sure who it was, they broke from the brush.

"By God, they raised hell," Galtry said, with a sweep of his arm toward the sullen red of the destroyed town. "Anybody else live through it?"

"We've seen nobody," Latta told him. "But there wasn't any warning, and I doubt there are many. We didn't even have a chance to arm ourselves."

"We'll look around." Galtry mused for a moment. "You boys had best go up to the ferry," he told Latta's group. "The Big Flat bunch is gonna try for the stockade, and if they make it this far down the river they'll cross there. Me and the boys'll look around a bit here, then I'm headin' for Crescent. If this don't get the army off its tail, I'll start me a war of my own down there."

Galtry and his scouts went on, and Latta's relieved party struck at once up the river.

Three hours later Latta found himself incorporated in a group of people who always before had shunned him, for old prejudices didn't count in this hour of disaster and continuing danger. From fifty to sixty people had arrived at the ferry above Elephant Rock. Others had scattered out to the undestroyed cabins on Big Flat to gather such provisions, blankets, weapons and ammunition as could be found and carried. Before the last of these had reached the ferry, too, the scouts who had gone part way with Luke Prine came back to report that the stockade so far had not been touched by the Indians.

"And we'd better hustle and get there," somebody said energetically. "It beats me why them redskins ain't jumped us already."

"They've had other fish to fry first," another offered.

George Murphy, the saloonkeeper, was a barrel-chested man with a heavy voice, and he was a good leader. The last of the company, frayed but too tired to feel much of anything at the moment, was moved across the river. Then Murphy harried them on along the nearly five miles still to be traveled. Only a few of them were mounted, nearly all carried a load, some a small child. Everyone had dressed up for the dance, especially the women. The little daubs of finery seemed pathetically ridiculous now. Latta saw Carol Dennis, still elegantly turned out but with a face drained and shocked into a graven image of her old self. He noticed Jody, who carried a sleeping child piggyback, but he saw nothing of her father. He estimated that by then there were about a hundred people in the aggregation, running heavily to adult males, of whom only about half were armed.

It took an hour and a half to reach the river mouth, following the north bank. Now daylight showed Latta the devastation that had been wrought on the opposite side. Smoke still lifted into the February air, wafting upward from heaped ruins of buildings and the smoking snags of trees. The women refused to look that way, and he saw the faces of the men grow dark and savage. He wondered how much Jody had learned or divined of the part he had played in creating that ghastly picture.

The company turned north, now following the Port Orford trail, up grade and down and having to stop often to rest. Latta heard more crying among the younger children, now, and he heard older voices grow quarrelsome. The stockade was about a mile and a half from the river, yet it seemed just that much too great a distance for the weaker of them to manage. Latta saw that some miner had taken the child from Jody. Now she walked alone, head bent. He had a feeling that she did know all about it, that she bore a crushing shame of her father's part in the disaster. He wondered what had happened to Jug-Up.

At last the weary procession came to the little open prairie back from the beach, where foresighted men had made preparation for this day. Slowly they filed over the drawbridge across the moat and through the opening in the high earth embankment into the stockade.

Still Murphy was a hard taskmaster, for he had the welfare of them all on his broad bachelor shoulders. He kept barking orders. Another thirty people had already reached the fort from land and mining claims north of the river. They all had to live for God knew how long in an area of scarcely more than an acre. The women and children were assigned one of the two buildings inside the stockade. The other, and the outdoors, would have to do for the far more numerous men. But shelters could be built from drift gathered on the beach, with fir boughs from the nearby woods for thatching. There was plenty of driftwood to feed the fires.

Murphy set up outposts on the prairie in an arc that had its ends on the sea, and the horses would graze within this half-circle. The food would be rationed carefully and shared equally, he stated, and all would help in the work of the camp. Ammunition would be conserved jealously. Each man would take his turn on guard and in foraging, as they must, if they were to hold out until help arrived from the outside world.

Then a miner who had been waiting at the stockade came up to Murphy and shattered what small satisfaction there was in the safe arrival of the company. "Me and Peterson come by John Geisel's cabin," he said dully. The remark riveted the attention of everyone in earshot, including Pete Latta. Geisel had lived north of the river, an area so far assumed to have been spared. "It wasn't burnt, but the Injuns had been there, sure enough. Geisel and his three boys're dead and scalped. We seen the carcasses. But there weren't any sign of his missus and the girls."

The lines of Murphy's round Irish face grew deep. Here and there a man muttered a curse. Nearly all of them knew the Geisel family. The boys were all under ten, and one of the girls was a baby. But Mary, the other girl, was about thirteen or fourteen, all but a grown woman. Nobody had to be told why the Indians had taken her and the mother, and there wasn't a thing they could do about it.

Pete Latta walked away from the group about Murphy, feeling a tingling in the back of his neck. Nearly all these people had danced while their friends and neighbors suffered who knew what horror at the hands of the savages. But the sight of Sebastopol and the fate of the Geisels had driven home the full, graphic horror of the situation in which they found themselves and from which there was no solid hope of deliverance. If they knew—Latta shuddered at the thought and wouldn't let himself pursue it.

He found Joe Durkin reclining on the slope of the embankment that ran about the stockade. Durkin was alone, surly, showing far too plainly his uneasiness about their personal situation. Latta sat down with him.

"Seen anything of old Johnson?" he said quietly.

Durkin shook his head. "But his girl's here."

"I know," Latta said impatiently. "I saw her, too. It's Jug-Up I'm wondering about."

He lighted one of his few remaining cigars, frowning thoughtfully. The Indians could well have gotten the old sot, for they had not distinguished friend from foe, and he hoped this had happened. Jody was not apt to betray her father, but Prine might be able to break the old man down and get a confession from him. Latta knew by then that Prine had gone to Port Orford for help. Prine might make it through the back, and if he did he would be spoiling for trouble.

In spite of his perturbation, Latta looked casual and relaxed when he rose and sauntered off across the compound of the stockade. Jody was on the back side of the women's cabin, by herself again, standing with her back to the logs and staring at nothing apparent with tired, dull eyes. She turned slightly when he came up to her.

Latta said quietly, "Where's your father, Jody?"

She watched him through a long moment.

"Dead."

"I'm sorry."

Even as he uttered this hypocrisy, Latta feared he would betray his relief. Now let Prine try to prove his charges, if he cared to make them on the basis of what some buck Indian had said to him in the mountains. Regardless of what Jody knew, she would not voluntarily expose to dreadful disgrace the man who had sired her. Not when she had already suffered from him shame in plenty.

Latta stiffened when he heard Jody go on in a deadly murmur, "Sorry? You've never been sorry for anybody in your rotten life. Not for Pa and the other people that died last night. Not for Mary Geisel and her mother. If you're sorry, it's only for gettin' caught in what come of your doin'."

His gaze sharpened. His last doubt was gone that she knew all about it. She seemed strongly enough moved to act care-

lessly of her own name and her dead father's memory. The
eyes with which she looked at him swam with contempt.

Unable to endure her scorn, Latta turned and walked away
from her.

7   LUKE STOOD on the prairie outside the stockade
on a depressing gray day of early March. Murphy was with
him, for the big Irishman had made him his right hand in
the vexatious, unending business of hanging onto life in
what had become known as Fort Miner. Luke's thoughts
were on the grim days that had passed since his futile ride
to Port Orford and his return empty-handed.

Although he didn't know what he could have done dif-
ferently, he still felt the failure of that mission. Instead of
returning with the help for which the imprisoned people
of Gold Beach had so vainly hoped, he had only added to
their worries. Yet he had had to tell them that they had
been left alone, the day after the massacre and for yet another, only because the Indians had been busy massing warriors on Euchre Creek, as they probably had done somewhere to the south, to cut off help from either direction.

Since then they had not been left alone by the Indians,
for twice war parties had swooped in to rake the fort with
gunfire from the edge of the prairie. There had been no
all-out attack, but one was inevitable and everybody knew
it. Meanwhile the Indians roamed everywhere in the area
they had sealed off from the world, riding stolen horses
and much better armed than their victims. All the buildings
on Big Flat had been burned now, and those north of the
river. Such foraging as the settlers could do was done in
the dead of night, and even so was highly dangerous.

Luke's thoughts were brooding on these matters when he
heard Murphy's heavy voice, subdued because of what he
said. "It makes my head spin, the grub it takes to feed so
many mouths. One meal a day they get, but I swear, Luke,
our commissary looks like it'd been cut in half every time
I look at it."

There was no use mincing words with Murphy, and Luke
said, "Do you think what I think, George? That Galtry
never made it to Crescent? If the Injuns put plenty of men
on Euchre Creek to cut off little Fort Orford, it's sure-shot
they'd put more between us and the outside where we could
get all kinds of help. This'd surely stir up the army, finally.

But even if it didn't, the people of Crescent would try to help us. I know 'em."

"Unless?" Murphy said with a lift of a shaggy black eyebrow.

"Unless Galtry never got through to tell 'em. George, I think I better try it, myself."

The Irishman weighed that for a moment. "You might have to, but not yet, Luke. We're makin' out. There might come a time when we need you and the way you know this country. A lot more'n we do right now."

Somebody called to Murphy, and the big man turned and went back across the moat. Luke stood there frowning, his eyes on a work party gathering driftwood on the beach. The two days respite the Indians had allowed at the start had been a godsend. During it, reconnaissance and foraging parties from Fort Miner had been able to operate in relative freedom.

Bodies had been found and buried until the toll of the dead now stood at twenty-five. Nearly everyone in the stockade had lost a relative or friend. Yet there had been happier discoveries. Foragers had returned to Big Flat during the respite and brought in more food and badly needed blankets. The unburned cabins north of the river had yielded more necessities. Several cows grazing in a back valley and overlooked by the Indians had been brought to the beachside prairie. Parties investigating the ruins of the Sebastopol stores had found usable tools and cooking utensils.

Luke turned and crossed over the moat. Dull eyes watched him come into the stockade, and strained faces failed to stir with even a mild curiosity as to why he had been outside. He stopped, looking about for Carol's face, although she spent almost no time outdoors and he was shy about going to the cabin of the women to ask for her. He was glad, though, that the women and children could be under a roof in the ocean-damp weather of March, although one end of their little building was piled with stores and equipment. In contrast only a few of the men could gain entrance to the second cabin at a time. The rest had to content themselves with the shelters they had managed to build and the fires that could be their one extravagance with a whole beach strip of driftwood at hand.

The stockade was fairly empty, at present, with the wood party out on the beach and the men who had been on guard or out foraging in the night now sleeping in whatever shelter they could find. A brush lean-to had been added to one side of the women's cabin for a place to cook. Some of the older women had gathered there at a fire, although the one meal of the day would not be until evening.

He hated to ask one of them to fetch Carol outside for he knew that some of them had come to criticize her among themselves for the pretty helplessness that made her a special concern to the men. But at that moment the cabin door opened, and Carol stood there, hesitating as if she were of a divided mind about emerging into the raw day. He grinned when her eyes fell on him, and she came on out.

The dress that had been so pretty the night of the dance was stained and wilted, and the slippers that had danced so lightly were muddy and scuffed. Carol had put a blanket over her shoulders, and a shadow fell on Luke's heart when she looked up at him with listless eyes.

Nearly everyone had a cold, and a few were down sick from overexposure to the raw weather, and he said uneasily, "You feel all right?" She nodded, and he added more cheerfully, "How about a little walk on the beach?"

Carol consented without interest and walked obediently beside him over the moat and onto the prairie. Her shock of grief, he knew, had been aggravated and set in her by the fact that the home she had found with the Kellys had been destroyed after so short a time and in such a brutal way, leaving her alone on the starkest and bloodiest of frontiers. It was not her fault that her upbringing had not equipped her for it. She was not to be blamed for the loveliness and charm that won men and alienated her own sex.

He wished he had the skill of tongue to tell her what lay in his heart, how in the months in which she had been happy in her life at Gold Beach he had dreamed of one day having her for his wife. How he had never quite screwed up the courage to tell her so. But he hoped she knew, as he had tried to show her since the uprising, that his one aim was to take care of her.

They followed along a path already worn through the drift and grass-matted sand to the blow sand and the tidal strip. He noticed that men glanced up to look at her, more openly now than when other women were around to notice. Carol must have observed this, for something gave her a sudden uplift of spirit.

"The sea's beautiful today," she murmured.

Although the mood over the surf was somber, the waves were gentle as they ran in on the sands. A noisy flock of seagulls stood at the edge of the water, as if huddled in some council of their own. Carol started to slant in closer to them, but Luke checked her because in the thin slippers her feet would soon be wet and chilled. They walked north, beyond the last of the wood detail but not as far as the last sentry post. A weathered log lay there, and Carol moved to it and sat down.

"I wish we didn't have to go back to that place," she said, putting the back of a hand to her brow. "The crowdedness, the smell, those pinched-faced women. I can't stand it, Luke."

He seated himself beside her, elbows on his knees, and looked at the sea. He knew that the spirit could rise to big things like hunger and danger only to be destroyed by little things that wore so on the nerves. There were times when he welcomed the risks of a night's prowling as a relief from the congestion and constant din, the litters and puddles of dirty water, the smells and embarrassments, the flares of temper, the complete lack of privacy, of life in such confined quarters.

"Don't let it floor you," he said gently. "A person can usually stand more than he thinks."

"You're not a woman."

"I know, but—"

"You're strong, and you don't know what it is to be afraid, and everybody likes you."

"Why, you're the belle of the camp."

"Not with the women." She shook her head. "I make the men remember how a woman can be when she's not worn down from work and going without and having their babies. And their wives know I'd be killed by the Indians rather than get to be like they are."

Luke thought that she spoke less in contempt than in fear that she would be forced into the lot that had made those women the way they were. Life had deposited her on this rude and lonely shore and robbed her of family, unprepared to make her way except through marriage. Which was all he could offer her, a marriage that would be little different from that of the settlers' wives on the land claims. He realized now that it was his fear that this was in her mind that had kept him from speaking out. It kept him from speaking now.

Yet she looked at him intently, seeming to invite something more from him, and he said, "I know it's hard to face, Carol. Mighty hard and wearin'."

"You like me, don't you?"

"You can't reckon how much."

"Do you want to marry me?"

The directness of it turned him speechless for a moment.

When finally he answered, he could hardly control his voice. "Why, there's nothin' I want more."

"Then get me through this and give me something afterward worth living for, and you'll have me. I promise." He yearned to take her in his arms, to kiss away her fears, to fill her heart with hope of the present and future. But she rose quickly. "I'm getting cold. Let's go back."

Walking toward the stockade with her, Luke knew she had only reached out to him in desperation, to have something settled to cling to in what for so long had been a grim and fearful uncertainty. He had been a good friend of Judge Kelly's, and that made him seem closer to Carol than any of the others with whom her life was now involved. Her uncle had considered him a man of promise in the new community, and she must have heard the judge say so. She had chosen him to be her escort in the peaceful months, and now she had picked him to save her from the fate she feared. It was so different from his hopes and dreams.

Before they reached the moat, he halted her a moment to say, "I don't need your pledge, Carol, to do all I can to get you out of this alive and well. It's only what I'd do for all the rest. But the other, something that's worth your living for, that's between you and me—between a man and a woman. I'll try to show you that something. It's for you to decide if it's enough for you to keep the pledge."

She smiled up at him wistfully. "If I can trust myself to you and know I'll be happy, you can have me any way you want."

They crossed the moat, and there by the side wall of the women's quarters stood Jody. Luke had a feeling that she would have ducked out of sight had there been time, and it seemed to him that she had avoided him, in particular, ever since they had been at Fort Miner. Each time he had glimpsed her, he had been aware of an inner turbulence that could not come entirely from the death of Jug-Up, shocking as that had been. He had a feeling that she knew her father's part in bringing on the massacre, that the weight of it was a heavy load on her heart.

Carol halted when he slanted so as to pass Jody, then hesitantly followed.

Luke said, "Howdy, Jody. I guess by now you must know Miss Dennis." Jody nodded, but Carol said nothing, and he realized that somehow he had created an awkward situation. "I never had a chance to tell you how bad I feel about your pa."

Jody nodded but did not reply.

He walked on with Carol who, when they came to the cabin door, gave him a quick smile and went in. Luke remained there for a moment, then turned back to where Jody still stood by herself. It surprised him to notice that she was a slighter girl than Carol, less tall and thinner in body.

He said bluntly, "Something's eatin' on you, Jody. What is it?"

She looked up at him and seemed about to deny his statement. Then she changed her mind and said dully, "You know Pa run guns to the Indians, Luke. I know now it's what you come to our cabin about, that morning when he was so boozed up. What you figured, that day, was right, but I didn't know it. He'd just got back from the mountains for Latta, and Latta paid him off in whiskey."

Luke let out a slow breath, for the first time sure of all he had suspected about Latta's despicable traffic. "When did you find out?" he said quietly.

"Pa wanted to die with a clear conscience. He confessed to me. He put it on my conscience to get it off his." Jody still looked at him, with eyes that brimmed with shame. "Latta's afraid I know and sure you do. If he can help it, he won't let you expose him to the people. They'd tear him limb from limb, the way they'd have treated Pa if he was here. Watch yourself, Luke. Him or Durkin, either one. They'll get you if they can."

Luke said sharply, "Has Latta threatened you?"

She shook her head. "I won't expose my own pa, and he knows it. But if you feel you've got to, Luke, I'll back what you say about it."

Luke stood stony-faced, his eyes glimmering. Ever since he returned to the stockade to find Latta and Durkin there safely, living and sharing the meager food supply with the people they had betrayed so callously, he had burned with the desire to call them to account. Before he learned of Jug-Up's death, he had relied on the old man, hoping to wring a confession from him that would convict the men even more guilty than he was.

Although he had suspected that Jody knew, he had not had the heart to involve her in the exposure and disgrace of her dead father. Now he had her voluntary offer to substantiate his charge, yet he could not take advantage of it, not at this point. Not only would the open shame be a mortal blow to her spirit, the people here would inflict on her, one way or another, the punishment they could not deal out to her father. It had to wait until the situation had changed somehow, so that it would be less painful to Jody.

He said gently, "Nobody ever faulted you for your pa's weaknesses, Jody. Least of all me."

"Blood's blood."

He didn't for a moment believe that, but there were too many people at Fort Miner who did. He said, "Well, I don't mind having Latta and Durkin sweat out the time wonderin' when I'm gonna call 'em to taw. But it won't be here, Jody. The worst thing that could happen in this stockade would be an explosion like that. It would probably end in a lynchin'."

He saw her face ease. Maybe she saw through that to the more personal fact that he chose to protect her, even at the cost of sparing Latta and Durkin temporarily. She gave him a faint smile, then, and he went on.

Neither help nor the promise of eventual help came from Cresent City, and the days of deadly monotony, of hardship and crowding danger, ran on through early March. The rains grew heavier, the cold air rawer, and nearly all of the besieged, particularly the children and old people, developed runny noses and hacking coughs and grew even more peaked of face. The larder shrank until there were only two beef cows left for fresh meat, with like shortages in the other simple staples on which they all lived.

Yet Murphy continued to deny Luke's requests for permission to try to reach Cresent City himself. The country was now completely in the hands of the Indians, discouraging even foraging parties, and the chances of Luke's getting through were even poorer than Galtry's had been. The attempt would be authorized, Murphy insisted, only as a last resort. Luke was not ready to defy him and act on his own hook which would be a precedent for a complete breakdown of authority at the fort.

By mid-March the occupants of Fort Miner were scraping the bottom of the barrel, and the men grew more and more reckless in their efforts to find food. Some of them, early in the siege, had discovered several bushels of potatoes in a settler's root cellar, and they had been nearly back to the stockade with them when they were jumped by Indians. So the potatoes had been cached near the mouth of the Rogue, the foragers fighting their way back to the fort. Since then, the river mouth had been heavily frequented by the hostiles, making the salvage of the cache impossible. Yet finally the shrunken food supply demanded that the attempt be made to bring in the potatoes.

On the night the decision was made, a party of fifteen, including Luke, Murphy and other men without dependents, slipped out of the stockade and moved down the beach toward the mouth of the river. It was to discover that they had walked into a cold-blooded trap. The hostiles had found the cache but, instead of taking the food, had set up an ambush and waited in the stoic patience of which they were capable for hunger to drive the settlers to try to retrieve it. Except for a premature shot by one of the lurking warriors, the white party would have been wiped out. As it was, a running fight followed, and by the time the foragers regained the stockade six men had been left behind them dead.

The disappointment nearly brought about a state of anarchy at Fort Miner, after all. Sickness was spreading among the occupants, as a result of the raw weather and the near-starvation diet, and there were no medicines. Since the suffering was greatest among the weak and dependent, the hardier men found the situation intolerable and began to plot a dozen different courses of desperate and independent action.

H. I. Gerow, who had been a Sebastopol merchant, came up with the most hopeful of these plans, and he and five others took it to Murphy.

"George," Gerow said, "them plagued redskins on Euchre Creek know by now that we ain't gonna get help from Fort Orford. And they ain't lookin' for us to try to get through to there again, so me and the boys figure we've got a chance to get by them." He nodded at his companions: John O'Brien, a miner, Sylvester Long, a settler, and Bill Thompson, Dick Gay and Felix McCue, who had sailed on the schooners in the summer seasons. "Syl's claim is up Euchre Creek way, and he figures he can get us past the Injun camp. If we make it, we can try comin' back by boat. Them three—" He tipped his head toward the sailors. "They know how to handle a sail in the open sea. We could get medicines, and there'd be room for a little grub."

Murphy was receptive, partly because he knew these people would undertake it with or without his consent.

The proposal served to restore calm and order, and two nights later the six men slipped away from the stockade and headed north. Long's familiarity with the country stood them in good stead, and they managed to evade the Indian camp and reach Port Orford on the second night. The northern town had recovered from its initial fright and was more willing to help than it had been when Luke made his appeal. A boat was secured and fitted with a sail for the attempt to breast the winter seas and make a landing in the surf off Fort Miner. The cargo was selected carefully and included the medicine needed so badly. In the dusk of the day of their arrival the wind stood fair, and Gerow and his five men cast off from the little port for the thirty miles of open sea between them and the people they had set out to help.

Luke was one of the party that waited that night on the beach off the stockade, feeding a brisk fire of drift to signal the boatmen where to attempt the landing. The outposts around the stockade had been doubled to prevent an attempt by the Indians, who would notice the huge fire, to interfere. Hardly a man who listened to the heavy grinding of the surf and felt the damp ocean wind on his face had any real hope of ever seeing the relief expedition again.

And yet, an hour before daylight, a faint shout carried over the sounds of the troubled ocean. The men by the fire sprang to their feet and ran to the lapping edge of the water. But there were no more shouts, and there was nothing to be seen in the muggy obscurity. They waited, breath shallow in tight chests, and then they waded to their shoulders in the water to see or hear better.

And then the sea gave up to them a broken oar.

The man who found it ripped out a cry that brought the others rushing to him. A breaker had left the bit of broken wood, where it spent itself and turned back, as a grim warning. Men ran along the shore for a considerable distance each way, but nothing else was found immediately. In the first streaks of dawn, however, the capsized boat, with its broken mast, washed in. Stronger light revealed the bodies of Gay and McCue at a considerable distance from the fire. The four other men had washed out to sea. The precious cargo had gone to the bottom, out in the swells where the boat had turned turtle.

The recovered bodies were carried to the stockade, where people gathered about them in silent homage, hearts cold and sick from the failure of so gallant an effort. Luke turned away to see Pete Latta on the edge of the group, his swarthy features creased in an odd expression of awe and cynicism. Moving up to him, Luke spoke quietly.

"Satisfied with your work, Latta?"

Latta started to reply, but at that moment they all heard the sharp, angry crack of a rifle shot.

8   LUKE SCRAMBLED to the top of the embankment, a
score of other men doing the same all along that side of the
compound. Even as he climbed high enough to see over the
prairie, a fusillade of shots rang out at the far edge of the
open grassland. He knew that the bright fire burning on the
beach all night had drawn Indians to see what was happening.
Unable to determine its meaning from the distance, they
seemed to have been worried into attacking.

Between him and the distant timber the horses and one
remaining beef cow were being hazed toward the stockade by the sentries, who stopped to shoot into the brush behind them and then turned to retreat in spurting runs. Even
as Luke took this in, a second volley beat out on the south
side of the fort. There was more than a needling party of Indians, this time.

Somebody else had the same idea and shouted urgently,
"Help get the stock on the beach, boys! Them Injuns
mean business, this time!"

Catching up the available firearms, men went over the drawbridge in crouching runs, the sound of shooting swollen by
then to a somber earnestness. But the sight of a half-hundred
men boiling out of the stockade was enough to keep the
hostiles from trying to advance across the open prairie. The
horses, with the flying-tailed cow, went shooting past the
fort and onto the beach. Instead of wheeling off along the
beach, as Luke feared they would, the animals stopped there,
wheeling nervously but not stampeding.

Settlers swarmed into the prepared positions that anchored
the fort to the water, breastworks planned to prevent the Indians from reaching the stock in an attack in force. Other
men had manned the embankment, where Luke had returned
with his rifle, and they kept up a fire that still gave pause
to the hostiles. Although the Indians began a taunting, hate-
ful whooping, they had dropped flat and were shooting from
fixed positions. The settlers covered the withdrawal of the
sentries. By the time they had all fallen back into the stockade or the positions guarding the animals, the northern sentries, so far unmolested, had also pulled in.

But the Indians were serious about it this time, as they
soon made clear. The grass of the prairie concealed them
completely as long as they did not move too much. The
pounding of the sea was drowned in the closer, sharper
crackle of the guns of both sides, the sound and hanging

smoke the only evidence of the combatants' exact positions.

Luke lay on the wet, sandy embankment with his rifle warm in his hands, like the others conserving as best he could the small supply of ammunition that stood between them and bloody death. Someone had rushed the women and children into the cabins and ordered them to sit or lie on the floor, beneath the level of the embankment top. Yet whistling bullets from contraband guns slammed into the log walls and ripped away stakes. Luke thought of Carol, his heart wrenched that this had to be added to the terrors she must endure.

Glancing along the embankment, he noticed the cool, oak-fibred resolution in the faces of the men he could see. There had been a great uplift of spirits in the last few minutes. So far in the uprising these people had been on the defensive, and for the first time they could fight back in spunky force. They watched the prairie grass that concealed an unestimated number of the enemy, waiting in steely patience. Then, when sharp eyes detected a target worth a bullet, the eyes would tighten, a hint of satisfaction forming about a hard mouth. Then the bark of another rifle would be added to the fury.

The savages, flattened at a lower elevation, made better targets than the men hidden on the foreshortened embankment slope. To close in the Indians had to crawl, stirring the grass in spite of their care. Some of the more bloodthirsty ones risked it, but the cost soon brought that type of advance to a stop. The Indians didn't have to take chances, for they knew what the settlers knew. There was only so much ammunition in the stockade. When that had been drawn off, there could be no more. After that, the weight of savage numbers would decide the issue in their favor.

George Murphy crawled along the firing line. "They can't scalp us without gettin' closer, boys," he kept saying. "Don't shoot at a thing unless you see it moving our way."

It was good advice but hard to heed for men whose nerves were keyed to the limit. Yet it was followed, although the Indians kept pelting the barricade and the lines that ran to the edge of the sea. For the first hour this was fairly ineffective, without a settler being hit, then in rapid succession Sam Tygh, boldly lifting his head for better aim, was shot between the eyes and killed instantly. His partner, startled by Tygh's dying groan, also raised a little and turned his head to see what had happened, and his jaw was shot away summarily.

Abruptly a voice rose on the prairie, where now what must be a hundred Indians formed a horseshoe about Fort

Miner, the ends of the arc touching the beach outside the settler lines. The speaker was some leather-lunged Indian who was haranguing his fellows. The white listeners could hear him plainly without understanding what he said, and they could only guess whether it was a plea to rush the settlers, to continue drawing off ammunition, or to withdraw from the fight.

Mouths dropped open when the voice stopped and the shooting broke off completely.

A voice next to Luke said elatedly, "They're gonna pull stakes!"

"Not," Luke answered, "without tryin' to run off our stock."

He had not been the only one to foresee that danger, for men all around him were risking their lives for a look. This drew a crackling of shots, which put an end to that. But the north side of the stockade had not been harassed. In a moment half the men inside the compound were scrambling over that embankment, dropping into the cold water of the moat and splashing and swimming across. Even as this happened, men on the outside lines began to bawl for help, for the shooting out there had brisked to a climactic intensity. The reinforcements joined them just as the Indians tried a rush toward the worried livestock. The white men broke the attack, turning back the savages in confusion. The animals rattled, then, and went thundering off, but to the north and away from the main Indian party. The only way to save them was to route the savages and keep them from circling the stockade and going after the stock.

Murphy bawled, "Charge 'em!"

A cheer answered him, and men boiled out of the crude breast-works. Most of the Indians were still falling back, and the charge was rash enough to unnerve such of them as saw it develop. Shrieks bucketed across the prairie, and in a moment brown, paint-smeared figures were streaking for the distant brush. The settlers were too wary to let themselves be drawn far from the fort, and they turned back. The stock had stopped a half mile up the beach and was quickly rounded up and brought back.

Depressing as the two casualties were, coming on top of the drowning of the boatmen, they couldn't completely dampen the uplift that had come to Fort Miner from having got in a lick of its own. The mood was all the more precious because everyone knew it could not endure. The food shortage had already been a worry, and now alarming inroads had been made on the ammunition. The Indians had only come in too weak a force, and over toward the mountains were hordes more of them for reinforcements.

Luke sought out Murphy and announced that he was leaving for Cresent City that night, concluding, "Don't tell me no, George, because I'd go anyway, and that'd be a bad example to the others."

"Yeah," Murphy said, rubbing his huge jaw. "That it would, Luke. So this time I ain't saying no."

Hunkered in a corner of the compound with Murphy, Luke suggested that, in order not to arouse premature hopes that might be dashed cruelly again, it was best not to announce the decision immediately. With over a hundred people in the compound, and the men coming and going, he might not be missed generally. Only if he was, should his absence be explained. He would leave the stockade with one of the usual night patrols, he said, on the pretext of scouting out the location of the Indians that had made the attack.

That afternoon the drowned boatmen were buried above the sea that had claimed their lives, along with Sam Tygh and his partner, with a simple but heartfelt service conducted by Murphy. Many people had died at scattered spots away from the stockade to be buried hastily wherever found, but now Fort Miner had a cemetery. The people who came back within the stockade walls after the service were soberly aware that the place of rest could grow rapidly now.

Luke, as evening neared, felt a growing concern about leaving Carol, perhaps never to set eyes on her again, among so much unfriendliness from her own sex. She needed a woman friend, and the only one who might be that to her was Jody. He was tempted to ask it of Jody, confiding his mission in her because he felt she could be trusted to hold her tongue. But he refrained through the day's one meal, eaten in the early darkness. Then he went through the usual preparations for a night patrol, saddling his horse and pocketing some of the precious shells for his rifle.

His decision came automatically when he chanced to glance up and see Jody watching him. She stood at a corner of the women's cabin, and there was an expression of infinite solemnity on her face engendered by the day's dangers and tragedies, all of which she would be holding against her dead father. He strolled to her, noting that nobody paid attention to them. He said quietly, "Keep this under your hat if you can, Jody. I'm headin' for Cresent and hope to get back in a couple of days with some kind of help. But if I'm held up, would you—well, sort of take Carol under your wing for me?"

"Crescent—oh, Luke." Then Jody surprised him by growing confused and dropping her gaze to the ground. When she looked up again, she nodded. "I'll look out for her."

"Thanks."

Luke walked to his horse, where men who were going a ways with him were ready to ride. A moment later the little party filed over the bridge onto the prairie. Once across the prairie, they rode southeast, watching the roundabout night, heading for a point up the river where Luke could ford the Rogue and go on south alone. This took them over high ground, thick with timber, and they had met with no trouble when, in something over an hour, they came to the river.

Luke shook hands silently, for even the quietest of talk was dangerous at that point. Then he slid his horse into the stream, walked it to swimming depth, and thus came, dripping wet, to the south bank. He was then at a point off Big Flat, now a scene of desolation, and from there he slanted to the southwest, not long afterward striking Trashberry Creek. He had had his own ranch at the head of this stream and knew the surrounding area thoroughly. He felt that he had a good chance of slipping through the region that was most heavily infested with Indians by taking that route, thereafter paralleling the Crescent trail rather than riding it. There was a slight wind, and his wet clothes had soon chilled him to the bone. Yet he was used to that from his countless days of all-weather riding in the express business.

His cabin and outbuildings had been burned to the ground. Luke stopped there long enough to scan the wasted site, wondering if he would be permitted to restore it and bring Carol there as his wife. The undamaged setting was still beautiful in the starlight, and when he built again he would plan for her, with every comfort and convenience he could manage. The work of a stock ranch was not the grueling toil of a farm claim. She wouldn't need to share it, even, if she preferred otherwise.

Luke rode on, leaving the valley and climbing to the ridge of a low range to the west. He made good time, for he was following a course he had used often to reach home without having to travel the long way around through Sebastopol. His body heat had begun to overcome his cold clothing and dry the sodden cloth. At times the upland serenity made it hard to believe that there was so much unrelenting hatred and violence so near at hand.

It was somewhere around midnight when he forded the Pistol, forced to swim in midstream, and he emerged drenched and half-frozen again. Some of the time he had spent merely waiting above the narrow valley until he was convinced that, through here, it held no Indians. Once over the stream, he quit the valley hastily, climbing back to the high ground. He knew that this time he would scarcely have begun to dry out before being required to plunge into the Chetco and then ascend into the cold air of the higher mountains, the Siskiyou range.

He rode steadily on, his teeth chattering again, his eyes aching from the endless search of the way ahead, along mountain ridges, in and out of canyons, only now and then having the open of an upland glade. The stars told him that it was only two or three hours from daylight when he came to the Chetco, well upstream from the regular crossing. Although he felt no warmer otherwise, his eyes had begun to burn from his intentness. Again he waited through long moments before dropping into the open valley. Then he descended, reached the river and went across at once.

Thereafter the high country was too rugged for him to travel the wilds without a loss of time that he could not afford. Yet he was across the Chetco, the last serious hurdle, and now he moved over to the edge of the mountains and turned down the valley, letting the cold horse warm up at a trot. With luck he could cut the regular trail to Crescent City by riding over a last ridge, where the river made a loop in its last lap to the sea.

His first warning of danger came in about half an hour when his horse flicked its ears and swung its head toward the river. The spot that interested it was at an angle and some distance farther downstream. Luke reined in, listening, and heard the far barking of a dog, whose outcries were being taken up by other dogs. An Indian camp. He wondered why it was this far above the ferry, which he estimated to be three or four miles farther down. A second village, probably, and the dogs would have Indians all over the valley before long.

He had to get past that camp and on the mountain trail before they could locate him. The noisy dogs would help him, for their barking covered any noise he would make. The horse shared his uneasiness and was soon at a gallop that required no spurs. Except for guiding it loosely, Luke let it pick its own way. The sounds from the village grew louder, passed on his right and began to fade. Then he was on the spur that would take him onto the trail and carry him quickly into the mountains.

9   IT WAS MIDMORNING when Luke reached a town livelier than he had ever seen Crescent City. There was a notable military color in the activity, and an unusual congestion caught the attention of his burning eyes. He had scarcely ridden onto the main street when someone hailed him in a voice of excited surprise. He turned his head toward the roofed porch of a general store. G. H. Abbott stood there, a Crescent man he had long known. Luke turned the horse toward him.

Abbott came out into the drizzle of rain that had started to fall at dawn. When Luke had swung out of the saddle, Abbott offered his hand, saying gustily, "I'm sure glad to see you, Luke. We'd started to wonder if we ever would again."

Luke tied his horse; then they moved under the shelter of the roof. Luke said finally, hardly daring to hope, "That sounds like Hy Galtry got through."

"Hy made it," Abbott said with a sober nod. "And died a day later from a bullet he picked up at the Chetco. You have trouble?"

Luke shook his head, saying irritably, "Well, if he made it, why in blue blazes haven't we had help?"

"The army again." Abbott shook his shaggy head. "Come and get a drink and some grub, and I'll tell you about it."

Luke nodded, and they started down the boardwalk, stopping first at a saloon, then going on to the Crescent House dining room. While Luke put away an order of steak and potatoes, Abbott filled him in on what had happened since Galtry's arrival had shocked the town.

Crescent City itself had responded with a whole heart to what the dying Galtry reported. Before the day was over, it had mustered into service a company of volunteers that had elected Abbott its captain. They had been ready by evening to leave for the stricken area, but before they got away the army stopped them. Captain Jones was still at Crescent City with a handful of regulars from Fort Humboldt. While he was himself greatly disturbed by the news from Gold Beach, there were plans that the Pacific Department was about to put into effect which he feared would be complicated if the volunteers took the field on their own.

"Plans," Luke said wearily, "they were about to put in effect when I asked Jones for help six weeks ago."

"Well," Abbott said with a grin, "when Jones showed me a copy of the despatch he'd sent the department, I said I'd wait and co-operate. It was hot enough to get him courtmartialed."

But it had got the army moving, finally, and on a scale large enough to accomplish something, which had induced Abbott to co-ordinate the volunteers' service with it. Captain Augur's company of Fourth Infantry, Abbott said, had been ordered to Fort Orford from Fort Vancouver by sea to join forces with Major Reynolds. Captain Smith had been instructed to leave Fort Lane with all available men and descend the Rogue to the Gold Beach country. Captain Ord's company of Third Artillery had been jarred out of its barracks routine at Benicia, and Lieutenant-Colonel Buchanan had been put in charge of the overall command. A week ago Buchanan had landed at Crescent City with Ord and his company. They were presently bivouacked with Jones' little detachment and Abbott's volunteers on the south side of town waiting to be mounted on horses that were being brought up from Arcata Bay.

"How long's that gonna take?" Luke asked.

"They think another day or so."

"Not soon enough." Luke climbed to his feet, his eyes angry. Briefly he told Abbott of the mass attack on Fort Miner by the Indians that had all but exhausted the ammunition. "They can't stand another, and one's comin' if it hasn't already. I'm gonna see this colonel."

"I'll go with you," Abbott said heartily.

He had a saddlehorse racked on the street and got it and joined Luke. Together they rode south through the town, Luke thinking that it was a pity word could not somehow have been gotten to the frightened people at Gold Beach that something so big was in the making. The cantonment where he had found Captain Jones on his previous visit had increased considerably in size. Luke saw the new, precise rows of tents that quartered not only the platoon Jones had brought from Fort Humboldt but the company of 3rd Artillery under Ord, recently disembarked from San Francisco. Across the road and a more familiar sight to Luke was Abbott's volunteer militia, seasoned frontiersmen who needed only a fire and a blanket to make camp. These already had mounts, picketed on a meadow beyond the camp.

Abbott led the way, and they found the colonel, who was with Jones and some other officers in the headquarters tent. Buchanan was not an outstanding man physically, and objectively he had the spit and polish of a professional army officer. He even had a brisk, cool way of listening, but he was attentive while Luke reported the dire circumstances to which the Gold Beach people had been reduced.

"We might possibly get away tomorrow, Prine," he mused, when Luke had finished. "We've got to mount the command, you know, and the supply train isn't quite ready."

"Tomorrow!" Luke snorted. "Colonel, I'd drop dead if you people ever done something today."

Instead of taking offense, Buchanan smiled. "I understand your sentiments, Prine, but don't be too harsh when you judge us. For some months Oregon's had a large militia under arms at federal expense. It was supposed to give you people protection, while we simply lack the men to garrison such isolated regions in proper strength. However, General Wool decided a couple of months ago it would be up to the regular army to put down the Indian trouble. But to decide on a campaign is not to be ready for it, believe me."

"I know," Luke agreed. "But how about Abbott's outfit going back with me? We wouldn't be far enough ahead of you to hurt, and those people up there need more than ammunition. They need to know help's comin'."

Buchanan mused for a moment. "Very well. But not till tomorrow morning. That shouldn't put you more than a day ahead of us."

Luke knew that was the best he could get and thanked the colonel. Abbott left with him.

They had reached their horses when Abbott said, "Well, I'm glad he cleared up some of the mystery. If the government's footin' the bill for the militia, you can't blame the army for expectin' 'em to do some soldierin'. But I'm glad Wool did decide he had to do the job after all." He swung to saddle. "You get yourself some sleep, because I'll be rollin' you out at daylight. You be at the hotel?" Luke nodded, and Abbott rode off toward the volunteer camp to get it ready to move out.

Luke yearned for a bed, but first he went to a store and bought a change of clothes which he took to a barbershop. There he enjoyed the all but forgotten luxury of a hot bath and a change to clean garb. Afterward he had himself shaved and his shaggy hair trimmed. He felt more like a civilized man when he returned to the Crescent House, took a room and prepared for the first real sleep in weeks.

Yet he crawled into bed, the shades drawn, to find himself too keyed-up to relax. He had expected to start back to Gold Beach immediately with help for his friends, for Carol, and here he was hung up in the slow methodicalness from which the army could not escape. He had had a good meal, a bath, barbering and change of clothes, and here he was in a good warm bed. His only response was a feeling of guilt and a keyed-up concern for those he had left behind.

Yet he opened his eyes to find the room dark as night, while daylight had filtered past the blinds when he got in bed. When he realized that somebody was pounding on the door, he knew he had slept a long while. He climbed out of bed and opened the door to find Abbott in the dimly lighted hallway.

"Throw on your clothes, man," Abbott said heartily. "We're ridin', at last."

"You bet."

Abbott departed after saying he would bring his men through town in half an hour. Luke dressed hurriedly, hungry again and wondering if he had time to get something to eat. He decided against it since he had to get his horse ready for the trail. Dropping down through the empty hotel lobby, where he tossed a dollar on the counter, he went out to a dark and rain-drizzled street.

In another fifteen minutes he was riding north with Abbott, accompanied by forty-three heavily armed men, many of whom he knew. They carried only light rations but were enlivened, secure in their numbers and foretasting adventure. Yet Luke had a feeling that they would have the ginger taken out of them before long, and he saw it happening even earlier than he expected. The trail onto the border headlands and back down to the low Oregon coast was slow traveling, winding in loop after loop and often threading dense timber. In spite of Luke's haste, the volunteers began to grow hard to hurry. The closer they came to the Indian country, the more reluctant they seemed to outdistance by too far the larger force of regulars that was to follow them.

The column stopped at noon to eat cold food from saddlebags, Luke taking his first of the day. The Chetco country, where he had had his worst Indian scare on the way to Crescent, was just ahead of them. There had been no sign of Indian activity, although that didn't mean they weren't onto this movement. A force the size of Abbott's would be helplessly spread out and encumbered, if jumped by Indians while trying to thread unseen through the high back country. And in sticking to the trail, they would run the risk of ambush, with it all but certain that there would be at least a sentry force of hostiles at the regular crossing of the Chetco.

"You're runnin' this outfit," Luke told Abbott, "but I think you better hold up while I scout ahead and see what's at the river. If we have to make a sneak crossing someplace upstream, here's the place to start it."

Abbott agreed, passed the word to the command, and Luke went on. He had chosen to go alone because, if the Chetco Indians had set up an ambush in the immediate area, they would not betray it by opening fire on a lone man. Yet he rode warily through the thinning timber and then onto the rolling but open lowlands. The command had ridden out from under the rain by then, but the smell of wetness and the sea was strong.

Close by the river, he left the trail and circled, gaining elevation and soon finding a viewpoint that let him see the ferry. As near as he could tell, it was deserted. The camp he had passed in the night was too far upstream for him to see its smoke in the muggy day, but he had an idea it was the base for the warriors guarding the vicinity. Either they hadn't tumbled to Abbott's presence, back on the mountain grade, or the size of the group had discouraged them from offering a fight.

He rode back to the company and talked it over with Abbott, Crook and Tuttle, the latter two having been elected the company's lieutenants. "That's where I figured they'd dispute us, but there's no sign of 'em."

"They skallyhooted for the mountains," Tuttle offered, "to save their own lousy scalps."

"Maybe," Luke admitted. "But I wouldn't bet on it."

Abbott gave the command to go on.

In spite of the peaceful surroundings, the slow approach to the river caused a tingling in the company's collective nape. But the crossing proved to be deserted, and the ferryboat had not been put out of business. Yet the little boat had been left on the far bank, allaying Luke's suspicion that the situation was a bit too inviting, but requiring a man to swim the cold water to bring the boat over. Then boatload by boatload, the horses swimming behind, the command crossed. That was their most vulnerable moment on the entire Gold Beach trail, and yet nothing happened at all.

Some of the volunteers attributed this to the theory that the Indians rose to no challenge greater than a handful of men. Luke didn't share that belief. Instead of belittling their courage, he reflected, it would be smarter to respect their cunning.

The command rode on for several untroubled miles, relaxed and cocky. Crook and Tuttle now rode ahead with Abbott and Luke, and they seemed to be as confident as the men that they had awed the Indians.

"This sure is fine country," Crook told the other lieutenant. "When we get the Injuns cleaned out, maybe I'll take me a claim."

"Fella might make a dairy pay on that pasture," Tuttle mused. "He'd have a market for butter and cheese at Crescent and Gold Beach."

Only half-hearing them, Luke lifted a sudden hand and looked about. But no investigation was needed to identy the sound that had struck his eardrums through the hoof beats and idle talk. Over on the right, a dense thicket ran beside the trail. The sharp, carrying bird call, which he had heard faintly because of his distrust of the situation, had come from that brush. Even as the command halted, the greenery gave forth the ringing shriek of war-whoops. Indians boiled into the open, a horde of them, most of them firing rifles but some nocking arrows to bows and whipping them in at the astonished volunteers.

Only the extended range saved the company from grave damage. As it was, two men were wounded, while Private Miller fell out of the saddle dead. The others wheeled their horses beachward, dismounted and tied the animals and then ran back to form a skirmish line across the trail from the Indians. They did not seem to be caught in too bad a position, Luke reflected at first. Rock and other natural cover let them form a front strong enough to break up the Indians' first whooping rush.

But they soon learned that the cover helped the Indians, too. All at once they seemed to have dropped from sight. Bullets peppered the volunteers' forting places, and now and then a winged shaft thunked in. But what worried Luke was the ease with which the hidden hostiles could surround them, cutting them off from the horses and even making off with the animals. He studied the surroundings, drawing a shot or shaft every time he lifted his head. Presently he spoke to Abbott, who passed orders along the line for it to fall back slowly toward the beach. If they could make it that far, they would have the sea at their back and could form a strong semicircle, using drift for barricades.

The volunteers crawfished a few feet at a time, helping the wounded to retreat with them. But they had not withdrawn a hundred yards when their movement was noticed and challenged from the rear. Some of the Chetcos had already got between them and their horses. Abbott swore and ordered the men to form a full circle, and Luke felt cold sweat run across his ribs. Water and rations were with the horses and such spare ammunition as the company had carried.

But the Indians didn't seem interested in the horses just now, believing they could take possession of them after attending to more important business. The Crescent City men were no longer cocky and fought savagely. They had all heard of Indian surrounds. Now they were caught in one and as badly in need of help as the besieged settlers they had set out to rescue.

The afternoon wore away without the Indians being able to overrun them, but Luke still felt the volunteers' chances would be better if they could make it to the open beach, and Abbott agreed. The captain crawled along the line, talking to his men. Shortly after nightfall, the Indian shooting dwindled, as Luke had told Abbott it would. The company probed forward and learned that the Indians had pulled back for the night, leaving only enough warriors to hold the white men pinned down.

The horses stood temptingly near, but the wounded men were too badly hurt to join the company in a break for the animals and a dash for freedom. So, helping along the injured, the volunteers moved slowly toward the sands. They drew shots from the Indian rear guard that hit two more men but were soon on the drift-piled beach. The Indians kept peppering them but showed no disposition to charge in their reduced numbers. Abbott's men worked frantically, throwing up breastworks of logs and sand, so close to the surf that their rear was no longer a threat to them.

The night passed, and the main body of Indians returned at daylight to find that their grip on the situation had loosened. The volunteers were hungry, thirsty, cold, tired and angry, and they soon convinced the hostiles that what had seemed easy pickings was going to be something else. Again the warriors dropped out of sight on the littered beach to begin the slower process of taking their prize by attrition.

The volunteers had no more than heated up their pieces when there came a sound more thrilling than any of them had ever heard. It was the spirited ring of a bugle tumbling over the lowlands. The volunteers cheered in their rifle pits while the tones crashed into the sound of the shooting. And then the Indians knew why they cheered. The commands of Ord and Jones, a hundred-twelve strong, came pitching over the rise to the south.

Shrieks followed the dying notes of the bugle, and some of the Indians shoved up only to be shot from the rifle pits. The savages squirmed on the loose sands, trying to breast themselves against an enemy that suddenly was on two sides of them. The regulars came on through a rain of bullets, sabres flashing, small arms spitting flame. Shrieks of challenge turned abruptly to the looser shrieks of panic. The Indians who could do so went bolting over the narrow strip of prairie and fled into the timber.

In a moment homespun men who theretofore had begun to despise the bluecoats were swarming among them, shaking hands and clapping shoulders.

"Damn my liver!" Abbott breathed to Luke. "Take them boys out from under the sleepy gin'rils, and they can get sudden, themselves!"

Even the higher ranking officers went up in Luke's esteem. Although he had left off his shoulder straps and had not been immediately recognized, Buchanan was in command. The horses had arrived at Crescent only a few hours after Abbott's company left. Leaving a detachment to bring on the supply train, the colonel had come on at once.

10   JODY THOUGHT she would crumble and die when the third night passed since Luke's departure for Crescent City without his coming back, with or without help. Now, on the morning of the fourth day, she could think of many reasons why he had only been held up, but they were not substantial enough to stand against her fears for him. She stood by the fire outside the women's cabin, her eyes dry and hot, weariness sapping her for she had not slept at all the previous night. She had tried to sleep, huddled under a dirty blanket on the hard earth floor, but at the slightest sound outside she had emerged. Yet none of the sounds had produced Luke, as her heart had prayed each time that it would. And afterward she had sat for a long while by the fire, which was kept going all night, sometimes with men who were wakeful for their own reasons, again by herself.

With so much coming and going among the multitude living in the stockade, Luke's absence had gone on a couple of days before it began to be remarked upon, requiring Murphy to explain it. The news had aroused mixed feelings in Fort Miner's prisoners, some swearing by Luke's ability to reach Crescent City if anybody could. Others had written him off immediately as dead already. Jody shared the faith showed in Luke, yet her heart was so wrapped up in him the fears of the others had taken deep root in it.

Abruptly she felt herself charged with a restlessness so great it had to be exhausted. The bridge had been dropped across the ditch, and she got to her feet and crossed to the open prairie. She expected to be called back, for women and children had been forbidden to leave the fort except in a man's company, but nobody's voice came rolling out to restrain her. The air out there smelled fresh and so clean, and she turned to the right, intending to circle the stockade and then go in again. Yet nobody seemed to have noticed what she was doing, and when she reached the west side of the fort she stopped, taking a look at the morning surf. The sea was calm, with hardly a cloud above it, and she knew enough about weather signs to realize that this promised a warmer day, maybe a sunny one. There was no sentries on this side of Fort Miner, and with a sudden rebellious daring she started down toward the beach. Still nobody called for her to come back.

For a moment she had an odd sense that nobody cared what happened to her, anyway. At best she was the daughter of what had been Gold Beach's chronic drunk. Yet she knew that this feeling came from her own sense of guilt, a self-pity she must cast off, and she came onto the sand of the beach and hid herself on the sea side of a drift log. It was pleasant there, so sweetly private after what she had endured of congestion for so many weeks. She sat on the sand with her legs straightened out, her back against the log, and watched the way the waves came stronger and stronger, climaxing and then starting the cycle over again.

Her nerves calming down, she could almost make herself believe that everything was well with Luke. Her mind drifted back to what he had asked of her the night he left: "If I'm held up somehow, would you sort of take Carol under your wing?" He hadn't realized how soon she would be called upon to do this, or to try.

Because he had asked it, Jody had kept half an eye on Carol and thus had noticed, when the day after his departure had passed without her seeing him, how visibly uneasy Carol became. She rarely went outdoors, letting Luke ask for her, but when evening came without his doing so, she emerged into the compound. Jody followed unobtrusively, and when she saw a genuine distress gather in Carol's strained face, she drew the girl to a vacant corner of the stockade. To that point she had considered her a woman of light and flitting fancies, but her obvious agitation suggested a really deep feeling for Luke.

Touched, Jody said gently, "Don't worry yourself about him, Miss Dennis. That wasn't a patrol he went on last night. He left for Crescent to bring us help. Another day or two, and he'll be here with it. So don't fret yourself." It was strange that she could feel this surge of tenderness for the girl who could make Luke's face light up the way it always did when he looked at her, the way Jody would have given her life to have it be for her instead. Partly, it was the discovery that Luke would not be hurt by her, that Carol really had feeling for him. For the first time she felt like using her Christian name and said, "He never told you because he hoped he could get back before you started to worry about him, Carol."

The strain in Carol's face gave way to a queer, preoccupied look of exulting. She hardly seemed to be addressing anyone when she whispered, "He did it—he'll save me— I'll get away from this horrid place—"

"Yes, Carol," Jody said soothingly. "He'll save us."

Her voice seemed to snap the girl out of a trance. Carol's head came up a little, and she said, "Us? Do you think he went for your sake?"

"No." Jody felt herself flush. "For all of us."

Carol smiled and turned and walked away. . . .

Jody was so intent on her thoughts that she nearly cried out when somebody spoke to her, right at hand.

"Good morning, Jody."

She glanced up, and there stood Pete Latta. He was looking questioningly toward the stockade, and when he smiled and sat down next to her she knew the smile had come because nobody had seen him out here, either. She wanted to get up and run, but his amused and cynical eyes held her still by their sheer insolence.

"You followed me," she said. "What for?"

"Why, I've always liked your company, Jody. And you needn't worry about gossip. I don't think anybody saw either of us leave. Pleasant, isn't it, to get away from that pack."

"Not with you, Pete Latta."

"Come, Jody." Latta's brown eyes gleamed. "That's no view to take of the man who could do so much for you." He no longer had a supply of cigars with which he liked to occupy his nervous hands, and they were restless hands, incessantly in motion. His swarthy, handsome face was now heavy with black beard, his shiny hair hung over a dirty shirt collar, and his expensive suit was smeared and in a place or two torn. Yet somehow he managed a look of grooming. The hands moved yet again, and he continued, "What do you plan to do if and after our long-legged hero gets us rescued?"

"I'll think about that when the time comes."

"My invitation still stands."

"What invitation?"

"To try your luck in San Francisco."

"In your company?"

Latta smiled. "And under my tutelage. You can't stay here any more than I can. It seems Prine shares your idea that your dead sire and I had something to do with bringing on the uprising. I think he intends to become very nasty about it when you no longer have to live with the people who'll despise you as Jug-Up's spawn." Latta smiled. "But don't get the idea that's because Prine's sweet on you. He's just a gentleman. Which I'm not, in the same sense."

She jerked away when Latta, deliberately and contemptuously, placed his hand on her leg. He laughed.

The lewdness in his expression, the cheapness with which he regarded her, were a shock. And yet she wondered why. Had her father not been a procurer for him, as well as a gun smuggler? Wasn't she blood of Jug-Up's blood, his spawn as Latta had called it? And Latta was right about there being no reason for her to stay at Gold Beach if they were not to die at Fort Miner, with every reason why she should leave. There was no reason why she should not do so with him, sleep with him until he got tired of her, then turn to other men. He had said she had a quality that made her desirable, in that way, at least.

He sensed to sense her sudden confusion, for he moved closer. She did not move away. She tried being Jug-Up's spawn instead of the Jody she had always felt herself to be. It didn't work. She could no more stand Latta's touch on her than she could stand his belittling tongue on Luke's name.

When he started to put a hand on her again, she slapped him resoundingly.

For a second there was a bright, angry danger in his eyes, then he smiled thinly. He eyed her in that alert, unyielding way for a long moment while she stared back in scorn. He got to his knees, and she thought he was about to throw himself upon her, yet she refused to show her fear. But he stood up and walked away wordlessly. Only then did she realized how stormily her heart threshed in her chest. He desired her, and now she had offended him deeply, and he would make her pay for it.

She sat quietly on the damp sand, her attention broodingly on the sea, until enough time had passed for her to go back to the stockade without drawing attention to the fact that she and Latta had been outside at the same time. She passed over the moat and back into the dreary clutter of human crowdedness.

She stopped at a fire where some of the women were warming themselves. They looked at her dully, without friendliness and yet without the thin antipathy they showed Carol. She was their kind, even if she had always been something of an outcast. A work party was leaving for the beach, carrying axes, to gather another day's supply of fuel. In the flimsy lean-tos others were asleep, men who had been on sentry duty the night before. The work party went over the bridge, and then a shout rang out.

"Hey—Look out there!"

It was not the kind of outcry that meant more Indian trouble; rather, the sound had held a note of glee. People in the compound turned and started hurrying to the bridge. Jody was across the ditch before she could see what had created the excitement. She gasped, her heart seeming to turn over from what her eyes beheld.

Along the beach trail from destroyed Sebastopol rode some two dozen men in blue uniforms. The thought struck her heart in ringing relief: soldiers. Luke had made it, was with them. She had located him already. Everybody about her was shouting, some jumping up and down in their excitement, but she only stood there, staring, weak in her gratitude. The party came on at a brisk trot, the riders waving greeting hands above their heads. Then a horse galloped forward, the one whose rider wore civilian clothes—Luke. He whirled up before the cluster in front of the stockade and swung out of the saddle.

"Luke—!"

The voice that called was a woman's, almost a shriek. Carol came weaving through the growing crowd, and she went running on to Luke. His tired face came alight, and while he looked a little fussed when Carol flung herself into his arms in front of so large an audience his mouth spread in a happy smile.

"You did it!" Carol cried gleefully. "Oh, I knew you would!"

Her hands pulled down his head and repeatedly she kissed his mouth. Even the women who had taken a dislike to her began to nod their heads and smile.

Jody looked at the ground but couldn't bring herself to go back into the stockade. The crowd grew hushed and listened closely to what Luke told them of the big military force nearly converged, now, on Gold Beach, of their deliverance, which he credited entirely to Hy Galtry who had died to do it for them. She heard Luke describe the bloody ambush at the Chetco and the last minute arrival of the

regulars, which had saved the volunteers from a very bad
time. Buchanan's command, Luke said, had stayed there for
a day or so to run down the guilty Indians. Abbott's militia
would make camp at the Chetco crossing to keep open the
supply line to Crescent. But Luke had been given this
detachment so he could come ahead and tell Fort Miner the
good news.

All the while Carol stood beside him, her arm around
his waist, head upturned, watching him, smiling.

11   LUKE SAT his horse where the river road came onto
razed Sebastopol's main street and observed the bustling
activity on every hand. A morning sun stood over the mountains, laying on the low-lands a notable warmth now that
April had appeared. It was surprising, he thought, to see how
much had been done in the ten days since Colonel Buchanan
arrived at the Rogue, bringing the remainder of Ord's and
Jones's companies from the Chetco, and the supply train
from Crescent City.

Now, as on every other day since the settlers were permitted to move here from Fort Miner, men were clearing
away the ruins of homes and business structures. East to the
army bivouac, south to the camp of the newly organized
Gold Beach Guards and west to the beach ran scores of
ramshackle shelters put up from salvage, poles and brush
brought in from the nearer timber by armed work parties.
Down at the river other crews were attempting to repair the
damage the Indians had done the "Rambler" and "Gold
Beach," although it would be weeks more before the little
schooners could brave the Rogue Bar.

The same urgency drove the miners and settlers. The
younger of these, especially men without families, had
gone into the newly formed militia company, hoping it would
help the army bring a speedy end to the Indian trouble. The
coming months were the vital ones, especially for the settlers who, besides making crops, had new buildings to think
of, new livestock to acquire, new supplies of food to gather
and lay by for the winter to come.

And yet, after the flash of action that had kept the ambush
of Abbott's company from turning into a disaster, the army
had relapsed into its snailing routine. Communications,
Buchanan told the impatient civilians, had to be established
with Fort Orford, where Augur's company had arrived by
sea from Fort Vancouver. More supplies had to be convoyed

from Crescent City, for the military had a civil population to feed almost equaling its own size. And Smith's company, which had been ordered to come from Fort Lane in the inland by way of the Illinois River, had not yet put in its appearance.

Luke was sharing a brush shack with George Murphy who, the night before, had said explosively, "Except for havin' a ring of army and militia around us and livin' on army grub, it looks to me like it's still a siege. Loosened up a little, which is a help, but that's about all."

Luke had agreed with the Irishman. The new civilian camp lay in the angle of the Rogue and the sea, with the military camps between it and the open country. No one could leave except in armed parties. Lumber for rebuilding could not be brought down from the sawmill at Port Orford, nor merchandise—and supplies for the saloon Murphy proposed to restore to the site he was clearing—from Crescent City as long as the Indians were pretty much on the loose throughout the surrounding country. There was a greater feeling of security than at Fort Miner, but impatience was becoming a mood almost as intolerable as fear.

Now Luke rode on through the vanishing ruins of Sebastopol toward the militia camp on the south edge. Yet short of there he swung from the main trail and followed another through charred timber and brush to the edge of the beach. The families had been concentrated in this vicinity, and he saw children at play on the beach and women going about the work of their primitive camps. On the ocean side of this area was the tent that had been furnished the two single women by Buchanan himself. Luke suspected that neither Carol nor Jody particularly enjoyed being teamed as campmates, but he was glad of the arrangement. Carol was almost helpless when it came to make-do living, while Jody was a good cook under any conditions and also saw to it that they had wood from the beach, water from the river, and drew their share of supplies from the army commissary.

Carol came out of the tent opening, the flap of which was tied back, when she saw him riding toward her. A smile came onto her lovely face in such marked contrast to the depressed and stolid expression she had worn at Fort Miner. The old light-hearted charm that had made her the darling of the male civilians had worked on the soldiers equally, and already she had acquired from them as offerings the wherewithal to restore her grooming: soap, a comb and mirror, needle and thread and buttons. She had washed her dress and looked as neat and fresh as she had before her ordeal.

"Good morning, darling," she said gaily. "How nice. I don't usually see you this early in the day."

He swung down, eager for the kiss he had coming and could now claim with assurance. She gave it to him with an arch smile, rising on her toes and rolling her mouth to his while she made a little sound of pleasure. It was so different from the early stages of their understanding, following her promise at Fort Miner when he had been so unsure of her true feelings. That had all evaporated after he returned from Crescent. Since then she had been openly and happily his intended wife.

They stepped apart, and he said, "Where's Jody?"

"Off somewhere," Carol said with a shrug. "She doesn't like me, you know." She narrowed her eyes at him. "Why? I thought you came to see me."

"Sure. I just wondered."

"What brings you so early?"

"The colonel wants me to go out with a patrol of soldiers. It's into country none of 'em's been in."

"Oh, Luke." Dismay doused the twinkle that had been in Carol's eyes. "Why you? Let some of the others risk their lives for a change."

"It's not much of a risk," he hastened to assure her. "Buchanan's worried about not hearing anything from Captain Smith. This patrol's just goin' up the Illinois and try to make contact with him."

"They don't need you like I do."

She was really upset, but it was one time when he couldn't humor her. He managed to say lightly, "Pshaw, Carol, it's only a little sachez over ground I've covered all by myself with the whole country swarmin' with Indians. This time I'll have a platoon of soldiers along."

"When'll you be back?" she said tremulously.

"That's hard to figure, but don't you worry."

"I will, and you know I will."

Her eyes reproached him, and again he drew her to him. This time she permitted him only a quick kiss, then pushed him away. When he turned to mount his horse, he saw Jody coming toward them from the main trail, although that wasn't the reason for Carol's sudden coldness. Jody had stopped, and he thought she would have turned quickly in some other direction, but she knew they had seen her. She came on slowly toward them.

He said goodbye to Carol, then mounted and rode up to meet Jody. He did not dismount. Her eyes were withdrawn and her tanned face locked. He said lamely, "I was just down tellin' Carol I gotta go on a little patrol, Jody."

"Good luck." Her voice was very small.

"Take care of her."

Jody nodded.

He rode on, thinking of the ineffective steps so far taken by the army to bring an end to the Indian problem. While preparing for more conclusive operations, Colonel Buchanan had set out to mop up the area around Gold Beach and gather as much intelligence as he could. The companies of Ord and Jones had done a lot of patrolling, without a challenge, making it evident that on the army's arrival most of the hostiles had withdrawn to the mountains. Yet a few villages of noncombatants had remained on the lowlands, the main one being up the river and just below the gates of the mountains. This portal being of strategic importance, the colonel had decided to move the village to another location. Ord and Jones were despatched to do so.

The two captains were informed of the exact character of the Indian encampment when their approach was met by gunfire that seriously wounded one of the sergeants. The joint commands flung out of saddle and returned the fire, which was too heavy to breast with a charge. But the Indians were fighting only to accomplish their escape. They slid out the open side of the village, across from the regulars, and were getting away in canoes before the captains understood it. When resistance stopped, and the troops stormed into the village, it was to find several dead Indians and nothing else. Anticipating that something of this nature was bound to happen, the rest of the village had left earlier, the Indian families moving up through the portal and into the mountains.

Although the treacherous village had escaped punishment, its misbehavior served to induce more truly peaceful villages to remove themselves from suspicion. One of these moved down the river to the edge of Sebastopol and petitioned Buchanan for protection from their hostile brothers and were permitted to establish themselves at Elephant Rock. Others fled to Fort Orford and asked for protection.

Meanwhile the colonel prepared patiently for a campaign into the mountains themselves. The companies of Reynolds and Augur were brought down from Fort Orford, more supplies were convoyed from Crescent City. When at last he considered himself ready, there was still the matter of the unreported Captain Smith from Fort Lane. So Augur had been ordered to go in search of him, with Luke acting as his guide.

The army camp's neat shelters stood by the river trail on the east edge of Sebastopol. Luke reached it to find Augur's detail, in platoon strength, saddled and ready to ride. He joined it silently, and the file stretched out on the bank of the Rogue, passing Elephant Rock and then crossing the river and afterward following the north side toward the mountains.

In late afternoon the column passed the deserted village of the treacherous Indians and went on. The river swung to the northeast above the village, and its valley grew chokingly narrow for a number of miles. This easily defended stricture was the mountain gateway, and the command grew hushed as it filled through. Above it the country opened somewhat again, and here was the junction of the Rogue and Illinois, a crude Y with the first stream on the left and the latter on the right. The Indian stronghold was on up the more impassable Rogue, while the Illinois angled sharply to the south, coming in from country somewhat removed from the regular Indian haunts. This relationship had let Luke cross the mountains earlier by way of the Illinois and caused Pacific Department headquarters to order Smith to follow the same route.

At the crotch of the Y, Augur halted the command and sat his saddle, looking up the Rogue for a long moment.

"So this is what they call the Big Bend country," he commented.

Luke nodded. "That's right."

"How far up is their so-called stronghold?"

"The lower end's about five miles from here," Luke estimated. "The stronghold itself runs upstream another ten or twelve. The chiefs keep their bands separated, you know. The last information we had on the coast put Tyee John on this end, with a chief they call Limpy at the upper end. Another they call George is somewhere between, and now Enos has joined up with God knows how many warriors."

"I understand John's the big chief."

"It was him that led the break off the reservation. But George and Limpy run him a close second, and we've had a taste of friend Enos. Like to pay 'em a visit, Captain?"

Augur grinned. "Not with an outfit this size. The colonel estimates that John's got around five hundred warriors, all told. What do you think about that?"

"Modest, if anything, now that the coast Rogues have thrown in with him."

To the troops from far-off Fort Vancouver, as Augur's were, the region was spine-tingling, and the detail was glad to turn up the smaller river and away from the mountain fortress. Yet it had gone on only a mile or two when the point riders saw ahead a small party of Indians, about a dozen, afoot, armed with rifles and formed in a sullen line across the trail. They were only a handful, and their insolence warned that other Indians, probably in larger force, were not far away.

The detail was still coming on behind Luke, Augur and a couple of noncoms and was too small to inspire fear in the Indians. For a moment the two parties only watched one another. Then, with a loud whooping, the Indians ran from the trail and disappeared in the brush.

Augur didn't have to confer with Luke to realize that his command was in a tight spot. If this bunch got away and reached a nearby camp, he wouldn't dare to take so small a force on deeper into the mountains. The danger to Smith's passage downstream would also be increased. Augur gave the order to charge, and the platoon went smashing forward. The Indians had by then found cover, but the captain's swift decision caught them before they could get set to fight. They put up a murderous gunfire, but the little command slashed through them, knocking them apart. Several of them were killed on the first pass. When the platoon wheeled to come back, the remaining Indians went shrieking into the dense undergrowth of the mountainside, where mounted pursuit was impossible.

Not a white man had been hit, but Augur's mission was seriously endangered. "What do you think, Prine?" he asked.

Luke rubbed his jaw. "Well, you don't know if Smith's even in these mountains yet. If you go on and can't connect with him, you might not get your little outfit back to Sebastopol."

Being of the same opinion, Augur ordered a withdrawal and left the mountains. Reaching the abandoned Indian village below the portal, which the hostiles had proved to be easy to defend, he halted and sent a despatch down the river asking Buchanan for reinforcements before proceeding with his assignment. Even in the improved situation, his position was precarious. The survivors of the clash on the trail would stir up a hornets' nest when they reached their own bases.

Pickets were posted, and the rest of the detail ate cold rations, not easy about the night soon to come. Afterward Luke called Augur aside and asked permission to make a forward scout by himself in the cover of darkness.

12   PETE LATTA was entering Sebastopol from the direction of Lattaville when he saw a horseman riding toward him at an easy gait. Recognizing Luke Prine, the gambler stepped quickly from the trail and placed himself behind the trunk of a tree, a direct meeting with Prine being the last thing he wanted. As he expected, the rider turned off the trail toward the family camp. Latta went on.

At the head of the trail Prine had followed, Latta stopped again. Down at the tent shared by the camp's single girls, Prine was talking with Carol Dennis. The lovebirds, he thought, his deep cynicism making the reflection amusing to him. He was about to go on when again something on the trail toward town halted him. This time it was Jody coming along in an idling walk. Again Latta stepped into the brush, deciding from her steady, oncoming gait that Jody hadn't noticed him. Jody turned off to the right where Latta expected, and he smiled when, at that very moment, Prine took the Dennis girl in his arms and kissed her.

Latta savored the moment, for it was no secret—except maybe to Prine—that Jody was wholly gone on him. The gambler's eyes gleaming when Jody halted, her lithe, splendid body stiffening. She was about to flee into hiding when the lovebirds noticed her, so her shoulders squared and she went on. Remembering the slap she gave him on the beach, one morning, Latta hoped that kiss had cut her like a knife. Prine mounted and rode forward, stopped a moment for a word with Jody, then came onto the main trail and turned toward the town.

Carol had gone back into the tent, and Jody went on by it, moving down toward the beach. Latta would have bet that this was a last-minute change of destination. He waited until Prine was out of sight, then on impulse he stepped across the main trail and started down toward the tent himself.

The flap was open, and Carol was seated on a cot that some army officer had placed at her disposal. She was running a comb through her long dark hair and had expected Jody. When Latta stopped at the opening, not speaking, she waited a moment then turned her head with a frown.

"Well—hello," she murmured, her eyebrows lifted questioningly.

Smiling, Latta removed his hat and made a slight bow. The arrival of the army had helped his grooming, too, for he had bought a razor from a trooper, a company barber had trimmed his hair, and he had soap for bathing and to wash out his linen. He felt stimulated, reckless, for this was Prine's intended, a woman Latta fancied he understood better than Prine did, himself.

Carol rose and came to the opening, returning his smile, and he knew she was extremely proud of her figure. She said, "Getting some exercise?"

"My walking is like your hair combing, Miss Dennis. It kills time."

She sighed. "And there's such a dreadful amount of it to kill. Do you think we'll ever live normal lives again?"

"From what I assume, you won't, Miss Dennis," Latta said smoothly, "even if they do get the Indian trouble settled."

She eyed him warily. "And what do you assume?"

"Partly what everyone does. That you mean to marry one of our local citizens and grow up with the country."

"And the other part?" she encouraged.

"That your life thereafter will be a far cry from the one you fit naturally."

"I suppose you can tell me the kind of life I would fit."

"Of course. One where beauty counts for rather than against a woman."

"Doesn't beauty count here?"

"Not nearly so much as the ability, Miss Dennis, to milk a cow."

She was both pleased and disturbed by his musings. For a moment she was thoughtful, then she said, "And what will your life be like, Mr. Latta, now that there is no Lattaville for you to be mayor of?"

"There'll be another."

Carol's gaze sharpened. "You're staying?"

"A while, Miss Dennis. I haven't quite gained the—shall we say competence that I came here for."

"I should think you've done very well here."

"Quite well," Latta agreed. "But my tastes are expensive. And I must get on with my constitutional. I noticed your tent as I passed by and thought I'd pay my respects."

She smiled.

He turned back to the main trail and went on through the town. He had been surprised by the speed and determination with which the other businessmen had set out to restore their enterprises and revive the town, at the will of the miners to return to their claims, and this had had an effect on his own attitude and plans. Oddly, the blow that was to have killed Sebastopol had really given it a new lease on life. If he was clever enough and made the right moves, he might lengthen his own period of prosperity here well beyond what he had thought.

He paused where the trail swung up the river, his eyes fixed on the stretch that was now lined by army tents. A mounted detail had formed up there, and Luke Prine was with it. Latta turned and addressed a man helping to clear the site of what had been Huntley & O'Brien's store.

Casually, he said, "Patrol going out?"

The man glanced at him and nodded. "That's what they say. They're gonna try and locate that bunch of bluecoats that was supposed to show up from Fort Lane."

"Prine's scouting for them?"

"That's it, I reckon."

Latta turned back thoughtfully and no longer strolled idly as he returned to the wickiup he shared with Joe Durkin, between the militia camp and Lattaville. Durkin sat on a stump outside the brush shelter, whittling on a stick of wood. He looked up at Latta sullenly. Since the lifting of the siege at Fort Miner, he had been anxious to dig up the gold and hit the trail to the outside, disregarding the fact that the country was still highly dangerous to travel.

"Cheer up, Joe," Latta said with a laugh. "We could be about to start on our palmiest days."

Durkin didn't look up from the keen blade of his knife. "Whatta you mean?" The servile respect he had once shown Latta had been lacking since the massacre, giving way to a surly contrariness.

Latta wished he had a cigar, for an expensive Havana between his fingers somehow added to his poise. "Prine's not going to be around to watch us for a while. It's a chance to make contact with Enos."

Durkin's eyes shot up then, startled. "You crazy?"

"We haven't milked the cow dry, Joe. Far from it. We're going to follow the example of our friends up the trail. We'll rebuild Lattaville. A more constructive undertaking, I must say, than all that damned whittling you do."

"You are crazy."

"Have I been so far?"

"Mebbe not till you trusted that Injun," Durkin said doggedly. "It's a miracle we never lost our hair. Or got our necks stretched by the settlers. Hang on if you're fool enough, but not me. I want my share of the dust." He nodded toward the ruins of the old saloon, down below them. "And then I'm shakin' the dust of this country off my boots."

"You're less of a gambler than I am," Latta scoffed, "and

the odds against making it through, right now, are too much for me to buck."

"Prine ain't gonna keep his mouth shut about us forever."

Latta smiled. "But we can make a liar out of him when he does do his talking."

"How?" Durkin snorted.

"By acting innocent instead of guilty. And it'd be admitting guilt if we cleared out right now, after which we'd have the law after us. Look, Joe. The fact that Enos didn't warn us about the uprising could prove a blessing. We were caught by surprise, the same as the others. Would we have been, if we were in cahoots with the Indians? Would we stay on in business here if we had cleaned up in contraband guns?"

"Prine knows about old Jug-Up."

"He only knows what some buck in the mountains told him. Hearsay of the flimsiest kind."

"Jody's suspicious." Durkin shook his head. "The old boy could've let it slip."

"Not unless he was too drunk to know better. Even flimsier evidence than what the buck told Prine."

"What's this about gettin' in touch with Enos?"

"I've levied an assessment against him. I'm going to make him pay for what he caused us."

"Huh-uh." Durkin tossed the stick aside, snapped the knife closed and dropped it into his pocket. Rising, he added, "I trusted your schemes once, but no more. Not me, Latta."

Latta shrugged, his mind made up about Joe Durkin.

He waited until past noon to be sure that Prine and the army detail were well up the river. Then, having eaten some of the beans Durkin had cooked over the campfire, he took a stroll up the river trail again. This time he went past the army camp and on over Indian Creek to the camp of the friendly Indians on the bank opposite Elephant Rock. Perpetually restless, he had walked up this far before. On a previous occasion he had recognized an Indian in this camp, a buck who had once sold him some Indian girls.

But girls were not his present interest, for he wouldn't need that income. Now, in addition to the former high-spending mining population, there were or soon would be several hundred troops in the vicinity. The soldiers were even more inveterate gamblers than the miners, and they had thirsts of at least equal intensity. As soon as the little schooners could go into service, he would import new gambling equipment and a whiskey stock, and meanwhile he could be getting a new building ready. The military would not object to it as long as he ran an orderly place. If they proved lenient enough, he might risk importing a few white girls later, for Indian women would not be drawing cards with all this trouble raging.

His plan was based on his conviction that the Indian trouble would not soon end and bring about a withdrawal of the troops. He had only to look at how quickly the military had slumped into its snailing pace after its dashing arrival. No, the army would be on hand for a long while, in which time he could add considerably to his fortune. The step he was about to take would help to make that a dead certainty.

The buck he wanted to see was known as One Ear, for something had happened to one of the windscoop attachments on the sides of his enormous head. Some urchins at play near the village told him that the man was fishing on a bar below the camp. Latta went on, coming upon a group of men dipnetting in a salmon pool below a riffles. One Ear was with them. He had once hung about Sebastopol and spoke broken English. Latta made a show of pleasure at the reunion, and then took the buck downstream and out of earshot of the others.

"I wish I could have brought you a gift of tobacco, my friend," Latta said warmly. "But you can see that I haven't any even for my own pleasure. Why aren't you in the mountains, One Ear?"

"Bad Injuns in mountains," the Rogue said grumpily. "One Ear good Injun."

"Come now, you're talking to an old friend." Latta smiled disarmingly. "I want to get a message to my friend Enos. I want him to know that my blood does not boil even though he failed to warn me before he dug up the hatchet. I think his cause is just, and I still want to help him with it." There still was no hint of interest in the Indian's locked features. "If he will help me do it."

After a moment, One Ear grunted, "How?"

"I want him to set up a way I can get word to him now and then. Like through you, One Ear. If I could tell you things the chiefs in the mountains would like to know, things an Indian couldn't hear himself, it would be a help to them."

"Like spy on soldier man?"

"Call it that," Latta said with a shrug. "I see and hear a lot more than you can, and don't try to tell me that isn't why you're living in this village. If I tell you something now and then, do you suppose it would get on to Enos?"

There was only a grunt from the Indian.

"For instance," Latta prodded, "you saw the soldiers go up the river today with Luke Prine. But you don't know where they were going and why. I do, One Ear."

Interest stirred at last in the massive face. "Where?"

"They're going up the Illinois because many white soldiers are coming down that river from the other side of the mountains. See? You didn't know that, but I did. Enos would have been pleased to know it in time to give them a welcome. Isn't that true, my friend?"

Latta knew he would never get a commitment from the Indian. With a friendly clap on One Ear's shoulder, he turned back toward the town, knowing he could do much to thwart an early end to the trouble.

He found Durkin in the shack, snoring on a dirty blanket thrown over a pile of fir boughs, his heavy, unsubtle face relaxed in sleep, his big body sprawled slackly. Latta halted in the doorway and stared contemptuously at the prone man. He didn't need Durkin and had only been testing his sentiments in suggesting that the man remain in Sebastopol. He knew Durkin had been to frightened since the massacre to consider that, and he knew what else was in the fellow's sluggish mind. Aware now that he would get no company, Durkin was stupid enough to think that he could undertake the escape alone, taking with him not only his share of the gold dust but all of it.

During the grueling weeks just passed, Latta had achieved a stoic indifference that had helped him curb his chronic wild energy. Now, with exciting new plans shaped in his mind, inaction was again unbearable. Yet somehow he got through the dull afternoon, spending most of it on the beach where he strolled on the tidal strip or sat and stared for long intervals at the sea. He went in to the wickiup for the day's last meal, and then dusk came in, the air chilling and a hundred bonfires coming alight.

Durkin built up a driftwood fire and, sharing it, Latta was aware of the unusual excitement, almost an elation, in the man which he tried to hide behind a seemingly changed attitude and a return to his old servility. Latta didn't give him an opening, so presently Durkin scrubbed a hand over his mouth.

"Where you gonna get men to do your buildin', Mr. Latta? Them that ain't workin' in the town have gone into the militia to fight Injuns."

"I'll offer wages high enough to get them. Why do you care when you won't be here?"

"Well, Mr. Latta, I been thinkin' it over. I been pretty buggery, but I guess it's like you said. We're safer here than on the trail, the way it stands."

"You're thinking about staying?" Latta said in mock surprise.

"Well, a while, anyhow."

Durkin's face tightened in a look of such poorly hidden slyness that Latta almost laughed.

Durkin was the first to go off into the shack to bed. Latta sat by the fire a while longer, as privy to the contents of the man's mind as Durkin was but doing a better job of concealing the fact. When he finally rose and went in, Durkin was snoring again on his pallet, this time with a blanket drawn over him. Latta took off his coat and boots, stretched out and covered himself on the other crude bed. He decided that Durkin's snoring was more industrious than usual. Latta lay on his side, quietly watching him.

It seemed an hour before Durkin stirred, turning his head to look at Latta. The gambler narrowed his eyelids. The big man watched for several minutes before he sat up. There was no motion in Latta except for the rise and fall of his chest. Yet Durkin took another long moment before he dared rise to a stand. With yet another glance downward at Latta, he slipped out of the place, his boots in his hands.

Latta lay smiling in the darkness, a hand searching the boughs beneath him. His fingers grasped what they sought, and he sat up and began to draw on his boots, hearing Durkin move off through the night. His boots in place, Latta put on his coat. He rose, and when he reached the door of the shack, Durkin was moving down toward the ruins of the saloon, stockade and cribs. He had a shovel that he must have stolen from one of the miners' shacks, such tools having been scorned by the Indian raiders as of no value. Latta's face kept its thin smile while he watched the big man fall to work among the ruins.

He'll have the site cleared, himself, before he finds the stuff, Latta thought.

Yet it took only a moment of spying for him to realize that Durkin had a better idea of the cache's location than Latta had supposed. Durkin was already at the approximate place, rendered uncertain of the exact location because the familiar interior of the saloon was now a meaningless litter. Latta himself was not sure of the exact spot. Durkin poked around with the shovel, and now and then he stopped to ruminate, then he would shift his position and start to explore again.

Sooner than Latta had expected, the man began to dig with a steady purpose. Latta's grip tightened on the hunting knife he held, which he had managed to steal from the salvage brought in to Fort Miner by foragers. He had needed it for confidence in the early days, against the Indians or against Prine or anyone Prine might arouse against him, without dreaming it would come into use in a situation like this one.

Within a few minutes Durkin bent and pulled something heavy out of the earth he had loosened. He put it aside and reached eagerly again, and Latta knew he had opened the cache. He felt a bright, animal-like enmity rise in him at the thought of Durkin's making free with his treasure, a nest of whiskey bottles filled with gold dust worth over seventy thousand dollars, as Latta knew from many a gloating session of weighing and figuring. The value was Durkin's present interest, but the weight was a problem Latta counted on to help righten the situation. It would wear out a horse to carry that much gold and a rider as far as Crescent City, and he doubted very much that Durkin had scared himself up a horse.

The big man finally seemed satisfied with his accomplishment and stuck the shovel in the earth he had laid bare of char and ashes. He had been lost in his excitement, but now he cast a quick look toward the wickiup. Seeming satisfied, he bent and picked up as many of the heavy bottles as he could carry on one arm. With the shovel in the other hand, he moved out onto the beach, so as to keep out of sight of the militia camp and its sentries. He moved swiftly and turned south.

Latta slipped away from the brush shack and followed to the beach. Durkin was still walking fast, along the tidal strip and well ahead. Then, nearly a mile from his starting point, the man turned abruptly and slanted across the blow sand to a low bluff. He stopped there, sticking the shovel in the sand and laying down his heavy load of bottles. Knowing the man would turn for another look to the rear, Latta dropped flat. The tide, he observed, was coming in.

When he raised up to look, Durkin was digging a hole up there, above the drift sand and well out of reach of the tides. Knowing the man would be tied up for some time, Latta moved to a log of sufficient size to conceal him. From there he could watch the beach, and in about five minutes Durkin returned empty-handed. Latta let him get well away on the Lattaville side and then moved up to another hiding place, this time the blind side of a large rock that Durkin had chosen to mark his cache. It would take the fellow three or four more trips to finish transporting his stolen treasure.

Durkin's slow mind must have labored long on the scheme,

Latta reflected while he waited. Horses were in short supply with both the army and the militia, and Durkin knew that if he managed to steal one, let alone two, he might have pursuit to escape as well as the Indians. So Joe was simply moving the cache, hoping to trick Latta into believing he had managed to take the treasure with him. Eventually, when the Indian trouble was over, Durkin hoped to slip back and pick up the gold.

Latta waited, drawing pleasure from the man's thick wits, while Durkin made three more trips. Then, after the final one, Latta's keen ears picked up the sibilant sound of sand being shoveled. At that point he began to move around the rock. Durkin, when Latta came in sight of him, had his back turned and was on his knees, smoothing out the sand with which he had covered the treasure.

Latta moved on a bound, his arm rising and striking hard. The knife seemed to meet with no resistance and bit to the hilt. A grunt gushed out of the back it punctured, and Durkin lifted himself a few inches before he slumped and sank to the sand. Latta straightened, leaving the knife in the wound, not even winded from the exertion. But it drew on his strength to pull the heavy body over the sand to a point a hundred yards away from the cache. There he removed the knife from the wound and used it to cut away Durkin's scalp lock. When found, this man would be a good example for those tempted to stray outside the sentry lines at night.

Latta returned to the cache, dug a second hole and buried the scalp, knife, and such sand as had been bloodied where Durkin fell. Then, on his knees and moving backward to the firm wet sand, he carefully smoothed out all tracks that the incoming tide would not obliterate. This was a better cache than the former one, easier to reach if he needed to do so in a hurry. Carrying the shovel, then, Latta returned to the ruins of the saloon and covered the digging that Durkin had done there. Then he went into the shack and to bed, at peace with the world and himself.

13   THE VOICE THAT challenged Luke was sharp in the night, sending blood crashing against his eardrums even though it spoke in English.

"Stand and be recognized!"

A man in the field uniform of the army stepped from the trailside cover into the shine of the stars. His carbine, raised to hip level, was lined on Luke, and his springy stance showed how tense he was.

"Relax, friend," Luke said tersely. "I'm Luke Prine, on a scout for Captain Augur and lookin' for Captain Smith. That your outfit?"

The sentry nodded, still jumpy and worrying Luke with the muzzle of his gun.

"Augur's got a platoon on the Rogue about ten miles below here," Luke resumed. He was comin' to meet Smith but had a brush with Injuns about five miles below here, so he turned back and asked for reinforcements from Sebastopol. Trouble is, it's stirred up the stronghold, which your outfit's still got to get past. I figured Smith ought to know and come ahead on my lonesome."

The sentry seemed satisfied, finally, and passed him on. In about five minutes Luke reached the bivouac, a rough camp set up on a riverside flat. Men sat about a score of small fires, their blankets spread for the night. Luke spotted Smith, whom he had seen several times at and around Fort Lane, and rode toward him tiredly, feeling the strain of the covert ride he had made since he left the old Indian village in the late afternoon.

Smith was at a fire with his officers and recognized Luke immediately. "Well, Prine," he said as they shook hands, "the last time I saw you, you were at Lane begging me for help. We're a trifle late, but here it is."

"A trifle?" Luke rejoined. "I'd call it considerable."

Smith sighed and described the punishing march undertaken, and not yet completed, by his command of fifty dragoons and thirty infantrymen. Horses were useless on much of the Illinois trail, so the detachment had moved on foot, under heavy pack, all the way from Fort Lane. The Indians had not expected a military movement along the upper Illinois and had so far given no trouble, but every other adversity had been afflicted on the snailing column. Smith's men were exhausted, their boots worn out, their rations all but gone. They had reached this point in an ill-founded rejoicing, thinking that another day's march would see them out of the mountains.

"I wouldn't wait for tomorrow," Luke warned, and he explained what had happened. "Maybe the Injuns don't know about you yet and are concentratin' on Augur, but I wouldn't take a chance."

Smith agreed and, tired as his men were, ordered them on a forced march that night. It paid off, for the situation proved much the way Luke had guessed. During the night the stronghold had teemed with activity, but the Indians were aware only of Augur's brush with the small party of hostiles and his subsequent withdrawal to the abandoned Indian village below the forks. Preparations had been made for a mass attack on Augur the next morning.

Yet when the warriors filtered down upon the village through the sidehill timber they were disconcerted by the sight of many times the number of soldiers they had expected to fight. Not only had Smith descended to join forces with Augur in the darkness, Buchanan himself had come up the river with Ord's company in response to Augur's request for reinforcements. The troopers saw Indians on the mountainsides and prepared for a fight, but nothing happened. When scouts probed the vicinity, it was to discover that the hostiles had slipped back into the mountain fastness.

So far in the lagging campaign they had shown no taste for a head-on collision with a large force. Luke and the more seasoned officers realized that this came from no lack of courage and fighting zeal. The Indian was at his best in guerrilla warfare, using hit and run tactics, nipping at his enemy's heels and trying to destroy him piecemeal. His technique of lightning slashes, with returns to a position chosen for its ease of defense, greatly handicapped an army trained to think and act en masse. The Army of the West had yet to forget frontal assaults and concentrate on separating the red foe from his base, dividing and keeping him on the run until he was exhausted.

When it grew evident that nothing would develop immediately, the fresh troops from down the river took over camp security, while Smith's hard-driven command got a skimpy meal and some sleep. Luke ate with them and afterward borrowed a blanket and stretched out on a sandbar. But he didn't fall asleep at once, for at last something seemed to have been accomplished, and it stimulated him. The long wait for Smith's arrival was over. The largest military force ever to enter the country was concentrated at the lower end of the Big Bend.

He fell asleep with the reasonable expectation that the back of the uprising would soon be broken. Then he could return to his ranch and rebuild it. By then the miners would be back on the bars and beach, the settlers on their farms, and he could start up the express business. Somewhere in there, he and Carol would be married, and that was a pleasant thought on which to drift off, at last, into deep rest.

"Prine—hey, wake up—we're going in!"

Luke opened his eyes to find Augur hunkered above him.

The officer had shaken his shoulder. With a groggy grin, Luke said, "Suits me, but I didn't think the colonel could move that fast."

"We're not going into the gorge, my friend," Augur said with a shake of the head. "We're pulling back to Sebastopol to sit on our tails a while longer."

"No!" Luke sat up. "Why?"

He listened in black anger to what Augur had to tell him. Smith had brought with him information that made his belated arrival of little consequence. The Oregon militia, officially the Second Regiment, was to play a part in the big push against the Indians by moving down upon the stronghold from upstream.

This force of nine hundred men, top-heavy with high-ranking officers, had been mustered-in on the heels of John's departure from the Table Rock reservation to slaughter and burn his way down the upper Rogue Valley and into the mountains. Cumbersome and mismanaged by citizen officers and territorial politicians, it had even been unable to keep John and his hostiles from raiding the inland valleys for horses, ammunition and supplies and harassing the trails. After several shakeups in the command, John Lamerick, from Jacksonville, had been given command with the exalted rank of general.

Since the turn of the year, Lamerick's command had been in winter quarters at various posts along the Oregon-California stage road, with regimental headquarters at Fort Vannoy. There the general enjoyed the prerogatives of his high rank and, as he frequently assured an uneasy populace, laid plans for a major campaign in the spring. For this reason he had not reacted too favorably to a request from General Wool, of the regular army, for cooperation in the campaign Wool had finally decided to undertake himself as the only chance of ending the Indian trouble in Oregon.

Lamerick's only response so far had been to assemble some two hundred men at Forts Vannoy and Hays. He had since then been readying them for an expedition down the Rogue as requested. But he had told Smith flatly when the latter came by Fort Hays that he would not be ready to take the field before mid-April.

"Squirtin' cuttlefish!" Luke exploded when he heard this from Augur. "That's another three weeks!"

"Make it a month," Augur said with a grimace, "and add a couple more for his really getting going and into position above the stronghold. But that's it, my friend. It'll do no good for us to start up the river until he's ready to start down."

The captain hurried away and Luke stood up, realizing that it was midafternoon. He couldn't believe that there would be more weeks of wearing inaction, with the lives of everyone at Sebastopol at a standstill, but Augur was right. Buchanan's hands were tied until the Second Regiment was set for a combined operation. But by the time he had saddled his horse, Luke had learned that the regulars were not all being pulled back to the base at the mouth of the Rogue. Smith's command was to remain at the old Indian Village to make it more .difficult for the hostiles to slip in and out of the stronghold. Supplies were to be sent to him as soon as the other units had returned to Sebastopol. And thus was spent the force that only hours before Luke had seen gathered here for what he had believed to be conclusive action.

That evening Luke was back in the wickiup he shared with George Murphy on the north side of Sebastopol. The Irishman had filled the air with blue smoke of his own at the turn of events, and it was news that sat heavily on every other mind in camp. It would be onto May, now, before the campaign could be expected to start. No one with the experience they had had with the Rogue expected a few weeks of brush fighting to end it. So the summer would be lost to them, and they couldn't go into another winter unprepared.

"If this don't kill us as a community," Murphy fumed, "nothin' ever will." His heavy, angry face was smudged with soot, for even that day he had worked with the cleanup crews. "What are you gonna do, Luke? Set around here and rot?"

Luke had grown thoroughly sick of inaction since the move from Fort Miner and had looked forward to action with the army. He shook his head puzzledly. "Dunno yet, George. Maybe the colonel'll loosen up on the restrictions and let us get on with things. He seemed to figure that leavin' Smith up there'll keep the Injuns corked in the mountains."

"Corked?" Murphy said with a snort. "Why, just last night a man was killed on the edge of town. Right under the noses of the army and militia both."

"Killed? Who?"

"That sulky jigger at the stockade. You know him—Durkin. Used to be Pete Latta's bouncer and handy andy."

"I know. You say the redskins got him?"

Murphy nodded. "Knifed and scalped on the beach below Lattaville. The colonel ain't likely to give us more freedom after that."

Luke agreed, but he was tempted to move out to his ranch

and get things started for himself and Carol, regardless. Murphy had had a crude meal ready when he reached the brush shack, and now Luke wanted to clean up and see Carol. He took the soap and towel they had drawn from the commissary and walked down to the river, his rebellious mood increasing. So far Buchanan had only asked the civilians for cooperation and to obey the rules he set up for their safety. Now he might have to declare martial law and enforce it with his troops if he was to prevent a mass exodus from Sebastopol, regardless of the Indian danger. The upshot of such a happening could be trouble as bad as anything they had experienced so far.

He washed up and was returning to the wickiup to put away the towel and soap when he remembered what Murphy had said about Joe Durkin's being killed by the Indians on the very edge of town. It was the first time the Indians had been that bold, and it was some satisfaction that Durkin had been their victim. Of the three white men guilty of gun smuggling, only one remained alive. If he waited long enough, Luke thought, the third—Latta himself—might wind up the victim of his own treachery.

He walked down through the half-cleared business section to realize that there was some sort of activity at the militia camp that had attracted a large number of the civilians. He went on in that direction to find that Carol was there, standing with a group of women on the edge of a crowd. They were listening intently to a bearded settler who was talking loudly and passionately:

"By doggies, it was us folks founded Curry County, and without a lick of help from the army. We come through the uprisin' and siege on our lonesomes, too. And now we don't need their army." Luke saw militiamen standing about who seemed in agreement. "I say, let's send our women and young 'uns to Fort Orford, and us men get back to our claims—or what's left of 'em. If we don't do it now, we might as well throw in our hands and leave the country."

"That's right, Alf!" somebody shouted. "It's that or starvin' tryin' to winter on a busted homestead!"

Luke sensed the dangerous mood in the crowd, which seemed to include nearly everyone in camp. Yet he shared it.

He came up to Carol and had to lay a hand on her arm before she grew aware of him. She turned quickly, then. "Hello. I heard you were back." Her coolness reminded him that she hadn't liked his going on the patrol. Now she seemed a little irked that he hadn't sought her out until now, after his return.

"Had to eat a bite and clean up," he said lamely. "Let's take a little walk."

"In a while. This man interests me."

"Come on."

His curtness surprised her even more than it did him. She gave him a keen, upward glance, then turned meekly and left with him. They were out of the badly burned area and moved easily through the clean trees toward the beach, coming down at a point where they could see the ruins of Lattaville.

Carol said, "Let's not go down on the dry sand. It gets in my slippers."

They stopped above a cutbank back of the beach, and a mild breeze stirred her skirts and teased her hair. He dropped an arm across her shoulders, and she let him draw her close but did not look at him. Something had changed in her during his short absence, resulting from his leaving her for the patrol or from the disgruntlement everyone felt from the prospect of weeks more of living under these austere, confining conditions.

He said gently, "It seems forever comin', I know. But we'll be livin' our own lives again, Carol."

She turned her head up quickly at that, looking at him unsmilingly. "But what kind of lives, Luke? And where?"

"Why, on my ranch. I wish I'd taken you to see it—that is, the way it was before the Injuns visited it. The prettiest valley you ever laid eyes on. I own a square mile. That gives me control of plenty of range to run horses and cattle. We'll live there, but I'll likely keep up the express business as long as it pays. I've always been a man to put by."

"You must have put by a lot in the years, you've been in that business." Her eyes searched his. "My uncle said that, being so dangerous, it paid handsomely."

"Well, that's right. I've got a pretty nice deposit with the express company. It'd be lonely for you, with me gone a lot, all right. So maybe it's time I quit that."

"Just living on your ranch would be too lonely."

His mouth jarred open. "You want to live here in town?"

She smiled and shook her head. "In San Francisco."

"My God, Carol—"

"I don't fit the life here, Luke. I didn't when I came here. You knew that. And I haven't changed."

"You're just upset—"

"No. I've thought about it a lot. There are wonderful opportunities in San Francisco. The business people are making the fortunes, not the miners." She smiled again. "With your courage and competence, darling, you could make a big success of anything you want. I know it."

"Well, thanks. But—"

She stepped to him, then, and slid her hands under his arms. Her upturned face was full of lurking promise. "You want me to be happy, don't you?"

"There's nothing I want more."

She rose on her toes and kissed his mouth. Then she let him take her in his arms and have a longer, more satisfying kiss. The warm touch of her had his heart jumping in his chest. None of the things he had wanted here equaled his want of her.

14   It seemed to Jody that, except for the children, she was the only one in Sebastopol without plans that were being held up by lack of action from the army. Sometimes she tried to make plans, thinking that she might somehow get herself another cabin. Then she might get credit from one of the stores they were trying to rebuild, so she could start baking again for the miners. Yet these objectives were not things that filled her with the others' fermenting impatience. Toward the alternative, to leave the country as she probably would—well, in that way the delay was an actual blessing. Until the trails were safe, leaving was out of the question. That let her put off the decision and the action, as she wanted, because while she was here she saw Luke, even if he rarely saw her.

But everyone else was chewing the bit in spite of the impressive proof that Captain Smith's presence at Big Bend did not keep the hostile Indians from going in and out of the mountains at will. The day after Luke's return from the patrol, a detachment of regulars had taken supplies to Smith. They had hardly started on the return to Sebastopol when the brush that skirted the river bank trail gave birth to angry shooting. The heavy volley showed that a large war party had set up the ambush, and there had been a brisk fight before the Indians were driven off.

So the weary settlers and miners postponed the idea of returning to their claims, and the Gold Beach Guards resigned themselves to more boring weeks of sentry duty at the civilian camp. And this had resulted in a disaster to a fishing party of Indians, friendly occupants of the Elephant Rock village, who were going down to the tidal flats in canoes. It chanced that some of the home guards had come down to the river to swim and wash their clothes, and when they saw the canoe party everything they had been holding in so long burst out of them. Opening fire from the brush on the unarmed Indians, they killed all but one man and two women, who swam to the far bank and got away. Eleven men and one woman were shot dead or drowned in trying to escape.

The upshot of the increasing fury on both sides, as everyone knew, had been that Colonel Buchanan sent Luke into the mountains again, to cross them this time and by way of the danger-frought Illinois. Luke bore a despatch to General Lamerick asking him to make every effort to take the field at once. Luke was to remain until Lamerick was in position on the upper Rogue, and then he would make his way back with that information, so Buchanan could move into the mountains after the hostiles.

Luke had been gone nearly two weeks, and it seemed to Jody a cruel magnification of the time she had waited for him to return from Crescent City. Hardest of all was that, during this new trial, she must share a camp with the girl he loved, doing nearly all the cooking and camp work, drawing their rations, bringing in their fuel and water. Not that she minded the work—she needed it to keep from losing control of herself. It was having to do this for a girl who could ask Luke's life and get it without, as Jody knew now, being worth his little finger.

On this warm mid-April evening Jody had the camp to herself. The thing that had so stirred up the animosity in her was that, a while ago, Pete Latta had come striding boldly along the path from the main trail and invited Carol for a stroll with him on the beach, it being such a delightful evening. To Jody's consternation, Carol had smiled and accepted prettily. So they had gone off up the beach toward Lattaville quite as if Carol hadn't a worry in her head about Luke's safety, let alone a feeling of loyalty to him. It didn't excuse her that she didn't know of Latta's despicable dealing with the hostile Indians, that she might not fully realize the kind of place he had run before the uprising. She was Luke's chosen, and to the girl who couldn't sleep nights worrying for him, her smiles for any other man were inexcusable, let alone her going off with him for a walk.

Jody chose not to be present when Latta brought Carol back, fearing she would lose control of her tongue. So she left the tent and went wandering up the path to the main trail and then turned without conscious aim toward the main part of town. The business section was now cleared of its dark ruins, although nothing could be done to raise a new town. Without conscious decision, she found that, passed through the town, she went on toward the river and the camp of George Murphy which was also Luke's when he was here. Murphy had just finished his supper and was seated on a stump in front of his wickiup. He greeted Jody with his wide Irish smile.

"Well, girl, I ain't seen you takin' your leisure for a long time. Sit down on the stump yonder. It's Luke's when he's home." Murphy chuckled at the fanciness of his furniture.

His cheery friendliness lifted Jody's spirits, but she had no idea of lingering. "Thanks, Mr. Murphy, but I was only gettin' a breath of air. Do you—do you suppose Luke got through all right?"

Murphy gave her a keen glance that made her flush, yet the question had been compulsive, as if the Irishman could give her some secret assurance denied to her. Murphy said, "Sure he did, Jody. Even the colonel knew Luke's the only man in the country, white or red, that can travel that country with his eyes shut."

"But all them hostiles—"

"He could lick the lot of 'em with one hand tied behind his back. You know that, Jody."

She had to smile. Murphy didn't mean all that, but if he could be light about Luke he couldn't be very worried. They talked a while, or Jody listened while Murphy talked. According to a despatch received by Buchanan from Fort Orford, he said, Joel Palmer had arrived at Port Orford by clipper. Palmer was the Indian superintendent for Oregon, and what he thought he could accomplish by coming here Murphy didn't know. Two-thirds of his dusky charges were holed up in the mountains and disinclined to listen to sweet talk.

Then some men came along and started talking with Murphy, so Jody left, turning back toward the family camp. Yet when she reached the turnoff she felt a strong reluctance to face another evening in Carol's company. So she sauntered on, although her shyness made her dislike passing the militia camp. Yet, while a few men she knew called greetings to her, she created no stir as Carol would have done had it been she passing by. Jody went on to the edge of Lattaville.

The site had been cleaned off completely, for Pete Latta had dumbfounded her by luring men away from the town merchants with higher wages, paid in gold dust, for the purpose of restoring his establishment. Even before the uprising he had been after her to go away with him, and at the stockade he had indicated that he would clear out at the first opportunity. And now he had become one of the stoutest advocates of the restoration of a town and community he had helped to destroy with his greed.

Jody turned back and at last walked down through the trees to the tent. Carol was back, apparently just returned, for she sat on a log by the coals left from the supper fire and was emptying sand from her slippers. Her cheeks showed the color that always tinted them so prettily when she felt good. Even her disposition had been sweetened, for she looked up with a casual smile. Only when her expression changed to one of amusement did Jody realize that her own face was an angry blank.

"So," Carol murmured, "you disapprove."

"If you haven't heard what kind of man Pete Latta is, you're stone deaf."

"Oh, I've heard the old hens gossiping," Carol said lightly.

"Well, if you don't care about that, you might think of Luke." Jody hadn't meant to vent her resentment, but it was pouring out. "You don't know if he's alive, but you're so little worried you can carry on with a man of Latta's stripe."

"Carry on with him? By taking a walk?" Carol threw back her head and laughed. "You funny goose. That's about as casual a thing as I can imagine, on his part as well as mine."

"Not on his," Jody said stubbornly. "He hates Luke, and he's hornin' in for the satisfaction it gives him."

"He hates Luke? Why?"

Jody realized that she had said too much, for she couldn't explain that antipathy. But Latta was not the main point, and she knew she could no longer hold her tongue on the real issue. In a small voice, she said, "Do you know what I think? You don't love Luke. You couldn't. The one you really care about's your own self."

The amusement fled from Carol's eyes.

"Well!"

"Luke's handsome," Jody said inexorably, "and before the trouble that was what you wanted. A handsome man to pay court and squire you. He's strong. And during the trouble that's what you wanted, a strong man to protect you. Now the trouble's ending, and I dunno what exactly but I think there's somethin' new you want. From Luke if you can get it from him. If not from him, from some other man. Maybe even Latta."

"You jealous little yokel!" Carol blazed.

"I love Luke, if that's what you mean. I have from the day I set eyes on him. But I don't blame you that way. I had my chance before you ever showed up, and he didn't want me. I don't think he wants you, either. Not what you really are, a woman who thinks only of her looks and clothes and what they'll get her from a man."

"You insufferable drudge!"

"I guess I'm that," Jody said. "But I had to speak out. You give Luke what a woman should or let go of him. Don't you hurt him."

Carol laughed and turned her back.

Jody left, going into the tent for her blanket, then turning down toward the beach. She knew that sharing the same camp thereafter would be impossible, but there was no other camp with a woman where she would feel any more welcome. She remembered hearing only that day that a patrol was leaving for Crescent within the next few days to bring in another supply train. It would be a large patrol because a good part of the freight to be convoyed was ammunition. Maybe the colonel would let her leave with it.

It had grown dark enough to draw in the last strollers from the beach. She reached the tidal band and walked for about a quarter mile toward the mouth of the river. Finding a place between two logs, she spread her blanket and stretched out for the night, more lonely than she had ever felt in a lonely life.

By morning her resolve to leave Gold Beach had drained away. All through the cold, sleepless night she had tried to picture herself in some other place, far away from Luke, and never did the thought grow less appalling. Not to know how he fared, not to catch an occasional glimpse of him, would be unbearable.

She chose to go hungry rather than return to the camp she had fled. Hiding her blanket under a log, she walked up the beach to the river mouth. Cookfires had begun to send their smoke into the morning air, she saw when she looked toward the town. Some men had taken quarters on the little ships, but none of them were on deck when she walked by. She kept moving upstream, close to the river and avoiding the army camp. She moved briskly, more for warmth than because she was in a hurry. Presently, for the first time since she had been driven from it by the Indians, she came to the site of the Johnson cabin.

For a while she only stood there, overwhelmed by the job of reconstruction which she had set herself. Although the mud fireplace still stood in ugly nakedness above charred poles and ashbeds, there was no other salvage. The shed that had sheltered her cow and chickens had burned, its occupants since having passed down Indian throats. There was nothing left her but memories. And they were not pleasant, for the strongest were freshest, of the night her father stumbled through the door with an arrow deep in his body.

Her eyes misted while she stood looking at the brush along the river that had given them a hiding place, where her father had gasped his last, repentent breath. She remembered the understanding of him that had come to her for a moment, there at the resurrection of the man he had been before the bottle became his master. She had known forgiveness there for a moment and, although a hardening had come afterward, she felt it again. They had taken to calling him Jug-Up, but he had been a man before he became a wreck, and then he had become a man again.

She turned back to the task confronting her and began to plan. It would be simpler and much easier if she selected a new site, but she needed that old, wide-mouthed fireplace. So everything must be cleared away from it. With summer coming, she could do her baking outdoors until the trouble was over and a new cabin could be put up. There were poles and brush aplenty along the river for a make-do shelter. Maybe Murphy would lend her the tools she would need. She would do what the townsmen were doing and be prepared to go back in business when the wherewithal could be brought in from the outside.

She fell to work and by midmorning knew she was a sight, smeared from toe to crown with charcoal, and dusted with stirred ashes. But she had cleared away the space around the fireplace and to her delight had unearthed her Dutch oven and all her baking pans, unharmed because they had been made to withstand heat. She had stopped to catch her breath, for the floating ash made her sneeze and cough, when she realized that someone was coming along the trail from town. Her reaction was feminine, an awareness that she was a mess, more than fear that it was someone from the military who would object to her being outside the limits of the camp. She moved hurriedly, putting the fireplace between herself and the trail.

In a moment she saw that there was only one person coming, and he was on foot. Fearful of coughing, she drew shallow breaths and moved to keep the chimney between herself and whoever it was. The passerby moved swiftly and went on up the trail. After a moment she moved her head enough to see, and the one watching eye widened. Pete Latta, on another of his walks. He was the last person she wanted to encounter out here, and she stood without moving. His figure shrank in the distance. It dawned on her that he was going to the Indian village at Elephant Rock, which she could see far off among the trees.

Latta moved with no great stealth, and probably this was only another of his restless excursions. Yet, knowing what she and Luke did of Latta's past dealings with the Indians, Jody was curious. She left her place of hiding and slipped down across the trail to the brush on the river side. The cover there was thick enough to hide her, yet sufficiently open to let her move easily. She began to walk toward the village, not entirely knowing why.

Ten minutes later she got the fright of her life. Latta had turned off the trail short of the village and gone down to a riffles where some Indians were fishing with dipnets off the rocks and off platforms they had built over the water. But Latta had stopped short of these, and she nearly stumbled onto him and the buck Indian he was talking with. Yet she stopped in time, still hidden but with her blood crashing so loudly in her ears it seemed that they also could hear it.

She knew that Indian with the big head and missing ear, to whom Latta was talking earnestly. They called him One Ear, and she had seen him loitering around Sebastopol before the uprising. There was no reason why Latta shouldn't stop for a word with him, but this was an earnest discussion, and even the Indian seemed excited. She turned, grateful that she hadn't blundered into them, and made her way back to her work.

15 LUKE CROSSED the summit a little before midnight, coast-bound again, the longest part of the Illinois trail behind, the worst yet before him. The inland valley, through which he had ridden the afternoon before, had laid warm and mellow in spring sunshine, but the night air was cold in the mountains. Yet the fact that walking, for he had been forced to leave the horse he had ridden from Fort Hays at a mountain ranch before crossing the summit, kept him warm enough. Also warming and hurrying him was the thought that he was going home at long and wearing last with word that Lamerick's bumbling militia was finally in place above the Indian stronghold.

It had been over three weeks since he came inland to find Lamerick slowly gathering his expeditionary force at the mouth of the Applegate, a little river that flowed into the Rogue well above the gorge and stronghold. The homespun general had laid his own plans for dealing with the renegades and Luke found him still indisposed to change them because of the army's urging. But the despatch from Buchanan did serve to inspire him to beat the mid-April date he had given Smith by a day or two. On April 13th the expeditionary force had passed in review before the general, a ragged, whiskery outfit mounted on horses and mules and armed with every kind of firearm.

The next morning, Luke with it, the impressive force moved out. A Colonel Chapman was in immediate command, and he rode in advance with a hundred men, two scout companies guiding them. A pack train followed, carrying twenty-five days' rations and a hundred rounds of ammunition per man. A Major Bruce closed the file with another hundred men, while in the rear trailed a herd of beef cattle. What the outfit had lacked in despatch, Luke reflected, it made up in thoroughness, for also in the pack were canvas boats for crossing rivers, shovels and axes for building roads and bridges, and certain equipage having to do with nothing but the comfort of the officers.

The route of the march had been down the south and west side of Rogue River, past Galice Creek and on to the vicinity of Peavine Mountain. There Chapman's command joined forces with the balance of Lamerick's regiment, which came in from Fort Leland under a Colonel Kelsey. The aggregate force, replete with colonels and majors as well as the general, amounted to five hundred thirty-five, big enough to plough under anything that could rise against it. By contrast, Buchanan's two hundred men on the coast looked puny.

The filled-out command had thereupon pressed into the mountains and it came upon nothing to plough under. A terrain of closely packed canyons, cliffs and towering ridges showed it nothing but a dense cover of brush and timber. Through this the massive aggregation threshed and floundered until finally it came to rest on an open flat topping a thousand foot bench on the north side of the river. Large numbers of Indians had frequented the place, but it was now deserted. So the command went into camp, around which it built breastworks. There was plentiful grass for the animals, an abundance of sweet mountain water and, while spring came slower to the high country, it was not too cold for comfort. The main force settled down while the spy companies tried to scare up some Indians.

Indians were easy to find this time, but getting at them was another matter. Three miles downstream from the military encampment was Big Meadows, where there had been a large village. But now, it developed, the village had been moved across the nearly impassable river and re-established on a bar on the south side.

But contact was more or less made, with the militia in place above the stronghold. At that point, Buchanan had requested, Lamerick was to have held fast while Luke hurried back to the coast by way of the Illinois. Then militia and army were to have entered the stronghold simultaneously and fought their way toward each other. But the militia general had no intention of subjugating himself to his army opposite number or of sharing honors with Colonel Buchanan. He ordered that the Indian camp be attacked immediately and annihilated.

His command would fight its way down the gorge, he explained to his numerous officers, as far as the terrain would allow. Then it would hold fast and permit Buchanan to drive the hostiles to it for extermination. Luke was ordered to wait until that final position was determined. The general went on to order Major Bruce to ferry the river with his outfit and get on the Indians' rear. Kelsey's battalion would proceed west from the bivouac, reach the highlands opposite the village and, wheeling, move down to attack it from across the river. With Bruce holding them against the river, the Indians' doom was sure.

Kelsey moved out eagerly, and luck was with him. Just west of the bivouac he ran into patches of fog that thickened and made an effective cloak for his command. Clinging to the high ground, he came to the point off the Indian village and there turned his column on a left face so that it formed a skirmish line when it descended to the river. Thanks to the fog, he could get down to water level and there lie doggo until Bruce had had time to get in behind the Indian village.

At that point luck deserted him, for the Indians had thought to put sentries on the north bank who instantly raised an outcry. Kelsey bit off a curse but had been given no option. So, with a resounding cry of battle, his command swept on into position on the river bank, facing the village on the bar across. Guns blasted the mountain serenity at the command to open fire; but all the Indians did immediately was to flee into the timber on past the village. This was not discouraging, for Bruce, when he arrived, would drive them back into range. While waiting, Kelsey's command riddled the emptied village and the brush beyond with bullets.

It soon grew apparent that the Indians were up to something on their own hook. While those on the edge of the timber held the militia's fire, other Indians were crawling into the evacuated camp and pulling back with packs. The militiamen did not realize that, however, until presently women and children, with packs, were seen climbing a trail up the mountain on beyond the timber.

"They're gettin' away!" somebody shouted. "Where in blue blazes is Jim Bruce?"

When Bruce did arrive, he was not behind the Indians, as planned, but on the same side of the river as Kelsey. Game as he had himself been in the attempt to effect a river crossing, Bruce's men had refused to risk their lives to the canvas boats that one bullet from the far brush could sink. Orders, arguments or entreaties could change their minds, and the best Bruce could do was swing down the river and throw himself in on Kelsey's flank.

Not that he wasn't welcome, for with their women and children safely away, the Indians had started to put up a scorching fire of their own from the edge of the timber that hid them. At the range, however, the main effect of the fire and counterfire was the shaking of the needles of the evergreen timber. The shooting on both sides grew less determined, but it was kept up through the rest of the day. At sundown the militia gave up and pulled back to the bivouac for the night. By morning the Indian village had disappeared.

Yet it had taken ten days more for the general to give up his ambition of ridding the gorge of Indians on his own hook. It was awesome country, and only rarely could the river be forded, yet it would have to be crossed time and again to find a passage downstream. Scouts tested it, and each time there were hostiles on the other bank, ready and eager to make a crossing costly. On the other hand, the Indians enjoyed a comparative freedom of movement. They knew every runway in the stronghold and thus could anticipate the militia's moves. Lamerick at last moved his command to Big Meadows, and he sent Luke back to Buchanan stating this position. . . .

Now Luke moved through a mountain night, coming down the Illinois again west of the divide. Not far ahead was Silver Creek Prairie and the camp of old Bearpaw, the Indian who had tipped him off to Latta's vicious trade with the renegades. Luke had left his horse there on the way out, and with it he hoped he could reach Smith's Big Bend camp before daylight.

He could see the morning star by the time he came down on the little prairie. By then a far-off dog had picked him up and was barking. But Bearpaw had been expecting him on his return trip for the past two weeks, and the dog abruptly grew quiet. Then Luke came in to the half dozen teepees on Silver Creek, where the doughty old Indian lived with his three wives and a proportionate number of offspring and in-laws. Bearpaw held a rifle, and his beady eyes keened the night until he was sure who was coming. Then he spoke in a guttural to the half-grown boy with him. The boy bounded off into the night, and Luke knew he had been told to bring in the horse, which had run with the Indian's ponies.

Bearpaw said, "How," and without waiting for Luke's return greeting clapped his hands. A squaw brought food, and Luke felt a rush of gratitude when he realized that they had been thus prepared for him night after night while Lamerick held him up. Bad Indians there were in the mountains, but these were plenty good. He ate the hot meat stew standing. By the time he had finished, his horse had been brought up, saddled for him. Luke slid his rifle into the boot, thanked his benefactors heartily and rode on again into the mountain night.

From there on he had to skirt the dangerous confluence of the two rivers, and he left the main trail and climbed to the ridges. The going was safer up there but much slower, and day was breaking when he reached Smith's outpost. Within minutes he had been ushered into a tent where the captain greeted him from his cot.

"Well, Prine, I gave you up for scalped about ten days ago." Smith grinned through the pale light of the lantern the corporal of the guard left on the rough table before he went out.

"Still wearin' my hair."

Smith threw back the blanket, disclosing that he had not removed many clothes for the night. He pulled on his boots while Luke explained the delay.

"I bet," Luke concluded, "that Buchanan's been chewing his nails."

Smith shook his head. "No. It made no difference how much time Lamerick took. And there was no good reason for you to risk your neck coming down the Illinois. You'd have had plenty of time to take the safe route via Crescent City. And go on a big toot before you left Crescent."

"I woke you up too early."

"No, I'm awake and mean it. Palmer's at Sebastopol. Like Lamerick, the Indian superintendent has ideas of his own for dealing with the situation. They include a new reservation, up north around Yaquina Bay."

"The Injuns had one already," Luke snorted. "At Table Rock."

"Which they jumped," the officer said with a nod. "And Table Rock was their ancestral home. Not a remote wilderness, like the new one would be."

"Does the man actually believe he can coax 'em in with that?" Luke asked incredulously.

Smith nodded. "To the extent that he's sent them invitations to meet him for a feast and a council. The date hasn't been set till he's learned their sentiments. But if there is one at all, it'll be the end of May."

"God Almighty!" Luke said bitterly. "Why, that's a whole month yet."

"During which time there'll be no military operations."

Luke shook his head dazedly. "This is sure some way to run a war."

The news left him weak. As a man of humane instinct, he would like to see a bloodless settlement. But things had gone much too far, and the Indians had been too successful in their defiance of white men's rule, for that to be possible any longer. He would be the first to admit that they had come in for some rough, unjust treatment from the whites. But it did not justify the savage butchery with which the ones like John and Enos had retaliated and which would continue until it was stopped by a superior force.

"What in blue blazes," he demanded of Smith, "makes Palmer think they'll take bait?"

"The military forces arrayed against them."

"Horse sweat. They've made monkeys outta the inland militia ever since they jumped the reservation. They just did it again to Lamerick, outfoxin' him and slippin' off with their thumbs to their noses."

"And a couple of days ago," Smith said, "I think they even shook the superintendent's confidence in his line of reasoning. They attacked an ammunition train coming from Crescent with a convoy of sixty men. And, my friend, they got away with a good part of it."

Smith went on to describe the attack. It was a mystery how the Indians knew that particular train would have ammunition. But they had known, and far enough ahead of time for a strong party of warriors to leave the stronghold and intercept it between the Chetco and Pistol rivers. The army had lost three men in the short but furious fight. While six of the Indians had been killed, with several more wounded, they had managed to get away with over half the pack.

"They've got good spies," Luke muttered.

"Excellent," Smith agreed. "Privy to Sebastopol gossip,

which is the only way that kind of information could get around. Some soldier going on the convoy mentioned it to a settler, and so on. But who down there gossips these days with the hostiles?"

"You think they've got a white man helpin' 'em?"

"That would explain it."

"Yeah," Luke agreed. "It would."

He declined an invitation to take breakfast at the army camp and rode on down the river through the growing morning. The nervous energy that had kept him going for weeks seemed to have drained out of him. The long wait for Lamerick to swing into position, if not action, had been all but unbearable. Now there would be another month of waiting while the Indian official got it through his head that, at this stage of the game, nothing could be settled by a powwow.

His horse had made a shorter journey than its rider had and traveled at a steady clip. Around noon Luke passed the Indian village at Elephant Rock. And then, just before he came to Indian Creek, he reined in, staring at what, when he left, had been the ruins of the Johnson cabin. Something had been going on there. A great deal of the litter had been cleared away. An open-sided shelter had been built around the still-standing fireplace. Walls woven of brush had made part of this into a closed shack.

Curious, he left the trail and rode up to the new structure. He had thought it deserted, but in a moment Jody came out of the tiny wickiup. The flushed confusion in her face told him she had tried to hide, thinking he would ride on by. He swung down, trailed reins and walked to where she had stopped.

"Howdy, Jody." He was surprised at how glad he was to see her. "What's going on here, anyhow?"

"Hello, Luke. Nothin' to speak of."

"You goin' back in the bakin' business?"

"Might as well."

"You been livin' out here?"

She shook her head. "They won't let me stay nights."

"Well. How's Carol?"

"I—reckon I can't tell you, Luke. It's been a while since I seen her."

Briskly, he said, "Is anything wrong?"

"Oh, no. We didn't hit it off, I guess. So I started this to keep out of her way. I been sleepin' nights at your camp. Murphy asked me, and I cook for him." She flushed, maybe because he might think her living there with a bachelor to be improper. She added, "Carol's been all right. She eats with the Updykes. And the men all see she has plenty of wood and water."

Luke had known how much waiting on Carol required, but he hadn't realized that it might have galled Jody to do it for her. Why had she done it, he wondered suddenly. Not for Carol's sake, from what Jody had just said.

"Luke?"

"You hear about the Indians gettin' the ammunition?"

He nodded. "Smith told me, up at the bend."

She shifted her weight, thinking a moment, then looked up at him uncertainly. "Well, there's talk. Some say somebody in camp told 'em it was coming in from Crescent and when. I haven't told anybody this, but the first day I worked up here I seen somebody go up to the village. It made me curious, so I followed through the brush along the river. I seen him and that buck they call One Ear talkin' off to themselves. One Ear and Pete Latta."

16   THEY WERE in the army headquarters tent, to which Pete Latta had just come, wearing a look of concern. "Like I told you, Colonel," he was saying, "I didn't think much about it till the talk started around camp about somebody getting information to the hostiles in the mountains."

"But the Johnson girl," Buchanan said in protest. "I've noticed her. Such a shy little thing, I find what you say quite hard to believe."

"I'm not trying to convict her," Latta said with a smile. "In fact, I hope I'm wrong. Under the circumstances, however, I thought I ought to tell you what I know and let you decide whether it's worth anything."

Buchanan glanced at a sheet of paper on which he had made a few notes. "Let's see if I've got it straight. Her father—I think you called him Jug-Up—sometimes did odd jobs for you."

"When he was sober," Latta confirmed, "and then only long enough to get the money for another drunk."

"You say he did some packing for you."

"That's right, but on a small scale." Latta shrugged and smiled again. "You've probably heard that I kept Indian girls at my place. I make no apology for it. This is a country of men without women—at least without many white women. There was a need which I filled, although that's hardly the point. The girls were the reason I sometimes sent Jug-Up into the mountains with a few pack ponies. The squaws simply didn't like white man's grub and wanted the kind they were raised on. So I'd send Jug-Up to one of the villages to buy jerky, smoked salmon, pemmican, roots, dried berries—that kind of stuff. He always wanted his pay in booze, and I didn't consider it my responsibility to reform him. I let him have it, a fact that his daughter resented and still does."

Buchanan nodded. "Then Johnson got the idea of blackmailing you?"

"Not long before the uprising," Latta agreed. "He threatened to spread the yarn that he was taking guns to the Indians for me. That it was how I got my girls—a gun for a good-looking young squaw. An ugly rumor like that could have given me serious trouble, especially in view of what happened. Jug-Up wanted ten thousand in dust. It worried me, but I refused him."

"And before he had done anything further, the Indians went on the war path."

"That's right, Colonel. The fact that I was caught in it, like the rest, shows how much of a stand-in I had with the hostiles." Latta laughed.

Buchanan eyed him shrewdly. "And Johnson's depravity led you to wonder if his daughter passed the recent tip to the Indians, as someone almost certainly did."

"More than her father's having a loose screw, Colonel. Jody's a very odd girl, as anyone who knows her will tell you. Never mixed with the whites, even before this trouble. Now she's all but moved out to where her old home was, all by herself. And close to the Indian village, Colonel. People despised her father, and it reflected on her. Maybe she's come to hate all of us."

"Well, thanks for telling me," Buchanan said musingly. "There seems to be a leak in this camp, and it's got to be stopped. We can't arrest her without real evidence, but we can keep an eye on her."

"Like I said, Colonel. I'm not trying to convict her. In fact, I hope I'm completely wrong."

He left, pleased with the results of his bold sally. It didn't matter in the least to him what Buchanan did about Jody. What did matter was that anything she or Prine could say now about gun smuggling would be discounted if not completely discredited by the military. Yet Latta had no intention of letting Jody get off with nothing worse than falling under military suspicion. He had not forgotten that slap in the face, on the beach at Fort Miner. This was only part of his effort to make her pay for it.

He strolled leisurely toward the main street of Sebastopol, where everything had come to a standstill as a result of Palmer's arrival and resolve to hold up the military campaign until an attempt had been made to negotiate with the Indians. Latta knew the hostiles were not going to be lured onto a new reservation with talk, however sweetened it was with promises. He probably had a more complete picture of their situation than any other white man around, Latta reflected.

Not only had they just replenished the ammunition they needed for the guns he knew them to have in good supply, but in the months since John and his band led the others off the Table Rock reservation they had captured several pack trains in the inland valleys, each yielding provisions. Valley ranches, on that side of the mountains, had been raided for food and firearms, while the squaws were experts in taking from the mountains and streams the food that nature provided. This was cached not only in the stronghold but at other points in the mountains to which the hostiles could retreat if driven from their present lair.

No, the war would not end in another month and maybe not in another year. So the army would have to remain here in force, resigned to protecting the area so the complaining settlers and miners could get back to their regular lives. Business for the restored Lattaville would be as brisk as in its palmiest days for that period.

He knew exactly the person to serve as his tool for the real punishment of Jody Johnson. Carol thoroughly detested her, now that they had quarreled over something—Latta knew not what—and Jody had moved off by herself. Carol had tried hard to justify herself after the split, without actually explaining what had happened between them. Latta, with his shrewd insight into the flaws of human character, sensed a need in Carol for the very thing he proposed to tell her. Yet with Prine back, and not apt to be sent off on another mission until after the powwow, seeing Carol was not as easy as it had been during his absence.

In his musings, Latta had come to the head of the footpath that ran off through the family camps to her tent. He turned, wanting to see her and with the thought that, should Prine be around, he could duck off unobserved. Yet Prine wasn't in evidence, and Latta found Carol on the back side of the tent. The sun fell fully there, and she was seated on a sandy bank combing hair that, he detected, had just been washed and was now being dried with care. The long, dark hair fell thickly over her shoulders. There was a cowlick on her temple, and a cropped strand of hair dropped over one eye.

She did not seem embarrassed to be caught at her toilet, only looking at him and reaching up to draw the comb again through her hair. The motion tightened the cloth across her bosom, and for an instant his breath was stilled.

She said with a slight smile, "Aren't you out early today, Mr. Latta?"

"I had business with the colonel," Latta said.

"Oh?" The tone she gave the word implied an instant curiosity, but he did not elaborate. She waited to see if he would, then added petulantly, "Well, I hope you told the colonel that I think he and the Indian superintendent are lunatics."

"No," Latta said with a laugh. "I only had some information I thought he should have." The cat's curiosity showed in her again. To whet it, he changed the subject. "Where's Luke Prine? After so long an absence, I'd think he'd be here paying court."

"He was here a while ago," Carol said, and he noted her indifference. "He said something about going out to the woods where they're cutting logs. Why they keep cutting them, I don't know. This dreary place is dead, even if they don't know it."

"I still plan on going back in business here, Miss Dennis."

"You must need money worse than I thought," she mused, "to cling to that in spite of all these setbacks." With that luxuriant hair loose on her shoulders, she seemed a slip of a girl, but there was wiseness in the eyes that regarded him in open amusement.

"It's not a need of money," he retorted, stung by her taunt in spite of his suspicion that it had been deliberate. "But the man's a fool who won't take more when it comes so easy."

"And when it no longer comes easy?"

"Then the enjoyment of it, Miss Dennis."

"How far off would you put that?"

"A day—a month—a year."

"Then San Francisco?"

"Lord, no. New York. Maybe even Europe." Her gasp told him so much that he felt emboldened and said with casual interest, "What caused the falling out between you and Jody?"

"You." Carol smiled prettily. "She objected to my being seen with you."

"How odd," Latta marveled. "I was just discussing her dislike of me with Colonel Buchanan. I sold her father whiskey when he had the money. Instead of blaming him for his drunkenness, she held me responsible." Latta shrugged and smiled.

"You thought the colonel should know that?" Carol encouraged.

"Not just that, but I'm afraid we've got into a confidential matter, Miss Dennis."

"You should have heard what she said to me," Carol said angrily. "Why would the colonel be interested in her? Tell me."

"Well—if you'll keep it in the strictest confidence."

"Of course."

"Well, I hope I'm wrong, but—" Latta hesitated, then repeated the things he had told Buchanan, not only of Jug-Up's attempt at blackmail, but the chance that Jody was spying for the Indians because she hated the white people. "But that's strictly a conjecture, Miss Dennis," he concluded. "You realize how unfair it would be to make charges to that effect without proof."

Carol did not answer. Smiling, Latta tipped his hat and left.

His only regret of the loss of Joe Durkin was in the fact that it left him to do his own cooking and camp work, tasks for which he had even less competence than taste. Yet he made out and otherwise enjoyed the days that followed his visit to Buchanan and, afterward, to Carol. He continued to move about, a habit so well established that no one thought twice about it anymore. And he watched closely and liked what he saw shaping up.

Having received no reply to his invitation to the hostiles to feast and council with him, Palmer sent out another message, his couriers being Indians drawn from the village at Elephant Rock. This message was blunter, dropping the suggestion of a brotherly feast and, in its place, pointing out the presence of powerful military forces on either side of the hostiles and the advisability of talking things over while there was time. He set May 21st as the date and fixed the place of the meeting at Oak Flat, some three miles above the mouth of the Illinois. This thinly veiled ultimatum was much more in keeping with the mood of the cooped-up settlers than the honeyed words had been. It helped them to find new reserves of patience.

Meanwhile, as the first fortnight of May passed, Latta had the satisfaction of seeing Jody Johnson become a total pariah in the little frontier society to which she had never belonged any more fully than he had himself. The slow-spreading malignancy had been launched as a confidence between friends—himself and Carol. Since it remained sub rosa, he was convinced that it had been spread in further exchanges of confidence. No one mentioned it to Latta, since he had no intimates.

His first proof that Jody had been condemned by the camp was when he chanced to see a settler woman cut her cold on the trail. It only added to his pleasure that Jody would not know what had brought on this change of attitude. It could be the fact that she, a single woman, was eating and sleeping in the camp of two bachelors. It could come from what she knew of her father's treachery. Or it might come, and Latta hoped she would remember this, from the fact that she had slapped the face of Pete Latta.

Yet in the last week before the deadline given the Indians, this hidden animosity reached a peak Latta hadn't intended. His first inkling of it was when Lije Balfour, a family man, appeared at Lattaville with an impressive looking document. A grimness in the man's eyes disturbed Latta, even before he spoke.

"Figured you'd want to sign this thing, Latta," Balfour said grimly. "We want to make it a hundred per cent."

"Make what?" Latta said with a frown.

"This petition to the colonel. He's takin' all the army and part of the home guards with him to Oak Flat in a day or so. We don't aim to be left here without defense and a spy among us. We want her locked up."

"Who?"

"That Johnson girl. Everybody knows she's in cahoots with the Injuns. It's the talk of the Goddamn camp. Likely she got 'em word the night almost everybody was at Big Flat and the rest got killed. We ain't gonna have that over again if we can help it."

"Nonsense!" Latta gasped. He hadn't meant for it to go this far. He didn't dare. Openly charged, Jody would tell the true story, with Prine to support it. Latta was fairly confident that he could weather such a crisis, after his talk with the colonel, but he would much rather avoid it.

"You want to sign?"

Latta shook his head. "Nothing as silly as that, and you'd do better, my friend, to tear it up."

The settler stalked off, and Latta knew the petition would go to the colonel with plenty of signatures, and Buchanan would have to take action. Latta cursed himself for getting carried away with his own cunning, forcing an issue that he might not otherwise have been required to face. Well, he had refused to sign their petition. That would be in his favor, too.

He cut short his usual evening walk, grown aware of an ugly mood in the civilian camp and a sudden open hostility toward himself. He knew Balfour had advertised his indirect defense of Jody by dismissing the petition as nonsense. He wondered what Carol would think, and even tell people in view of what he had told her of Jody's suspicious behavior. He returned to his wickiup and, shortly after nightfall, went to bed.

When he awakened, it was with a heart-pounding start. A voice, guttural, low but carrying, was saying, "Latta—Pete Latta—" He saw the dim, blanket-draped figure in the doorway, the old slouch hat on the oversized head above it.

"One Ear!" He gasped. "Are you crazy? Get out of here!"

"One Ear bring word, Pete Latta. From Enos. He want to know how many soldier mans come into mountains with Palmer, how many stay here."

Latta's blood ran cold at the implication. Just what the settlers feared! Enos, unless the force left on guard here was strong enough to discourage him, meant to attempt another massacre while the main body of troops was at the council.

"No!" he protested. "He can't do it!"

"You say Pete Latta friend of Enos," said the flat, insistent voice. "You tell him about shells on mules for guns. You trade plenty guns and get squaws for jig-jig house. You not his friend now, Pete Latta?"

"Of course I am!" Latta assured him. "And I'm being his friend when I tell him not to attack this place again. They expect it. They'll set a trap and he and his braves will all be killed. Go back and tell him I send him that word as his old and trusted friend."

The next sound fairly curdled the blood that ran so cold in Latta's veins. It was just outside and said briskly, "That's enough, One Ear. You really *are* a good Injun with a rifle at your back. Step out now, and you follow him, Latta."

"Prine," Latta said in a spent voice.

"There's enough men out here to shoot your wickiup to pieces. I'm countin' to three."

Latta pushed up, hardly able to stand, and stumbled to the doorway. The Indian had drawn back, but the barrel of Prine's rifle was shoved against his spine. Latta's faint hope of bluffing it out died when he saw Buchanan there, two

114

other officers with him, and Balfour, the settler who had circulated the petition.

"You hear enough, Colonel?" Prine said.

"Plenty." Buchanan turned to the settler. "And you, Mr. Balfour, shall have the arrest your petition asks for. But it will be the real traitor."

17 THREE MONTHS to the day after the massacre, Sebastopol stirred at last to the excitement of something fittingly retaliatory and conclusive being done. Opinions were mixed as to what the outcome of the council would be, some stubbornly hoping a peaceful settlement might emerge, most doubting that the hostiles would come to Oak Flat at all. But if they did not come, everyone knew, the army was committed to fitting action, for it would not permit its ultimatum to be ignored.

Smith had already been ordered to proceed on up the river from the old Indian village and station himself and company at Oak Flat. Behind him, out of Sebastopol, went the companies of Jones, Reynolds and Augur, and part of the Gold Beach Guards. Captain Ord and company would also join them, but at present Ord was bringing a supply train to the flat from Port Orford. Palmer, the Indian agent, and Colonel Buchanan were the last to leave for the mountains, planning to reach the flat only a day before the council was to be held.

Luke had wanted to attach himself to the Guards for the occasion, but the colonel had asked him to wait and accompany him and Palmer, neither of whom had been that far up the river. Thus Luke found himself still in a camp that seemed strangely empty and exposed, although the civilian population had not been diminished except for some of the militia company.

He and Murphy had finished supper when the Irishman said complainingly, "I wish that boogery yarn about Enos had never got started. It don't make sense, but, by gum, I can't get it outta my head."

Luke knew that went for nearly everybody left behind. It was improbable that even an Indian as bold as Enos would try anything so reckless as raiding the town again, yet the possibility was there. It had been cogent enough to rattle Latta and smoke him out, at last. The gambler had Jody to thank for his downfall. If she hadn't been suspicious when she saw him going to the Indian village, it would have been impossible to expose him so neatly. It had been a terrible time for Jody, and Luke still didn't know how the malicious talk about her had got started. But the way she had borne it had opened his eyes anew to the steel in the spine of her pretty back, to the oak in her shy heart. And it had brought him face to face with an awareness that was on his mind now. There was a painful thing he had to do before he left for the mountains.

He put it off until twilight began to settle in, then rose and walked down through the scattered camps to Carol's tent. She had been strangely demure and self-contained, the last few days, and hardly seemed glad to see him. But he sat down with her at her fire, and after a moment said quietly, "You still want to leave this country after the trouble's settled?"

"Yes."

"Well, it's only fair to tell you that I figure my life is here."

"I know that."

"Is it all right with you?"

She didn't answer him.

He had nothing further to say, yet he sat there a while with her, wondering what had happened to the enchantment that so long had filled him in her company. He waited for her to break the pledge between them if she wanted, and when she did not, he rose, saying, "Well, I'll be back in a few days." She nodded and he left.

It was midafternoon, the next day, when Luke arrived with Joel Palmer and Colonel Buchanan at Oak Flat to find a most impressive display of military might. Over two hundred strong they were, yet the night before the appointed council held an undertone of deep uneasiness which robbed the big command of sleep. They all knew that white forces had fought John and his warriors for nearly six years, counting the original inland campaign that had put him on the Table Rock reservation in the first place. They knew that Enos was a completely wild fanatic. The troops had reached the mountains in high spirits, but in the black night it seemed a lot to expect that the thing could end from a little talk.

When bugles shook the mountain stillness in the first light of the day of the deadline, the command rolled from its blankets without the noisy good humor of the days before and cooked and ate hurried breakfasts at a hundred small fires. Buchanan and Palmer waited silently, tensely, the officer wanting to bring his mission to a successful end, the superintendent—a devout man—longing to spare his red charges the fury that might have to be loosed upon them.

No one offered a bet on whether the Indians would come, yet in midmorning they did come, only the head men as had been stipulated. These had been allowed to keep their arms, and Luke knew that their warriors would not be far in the distance. He felt uneasiness riffle through the command, whose eyes riveted on the gaunt, gray Indian with the charcoal eyes that they all knew to be the famous John. He was ragged, and his braids hung limply across a sagging chest, but there was a dignity there that canceled any impulse to despite him for a savage. There was a lame chief who had to be Limpy, Luke thought, and most of the volunteers recognized Enos. Lesser chiefs made up the entourage Some of them, like Enos, had not long before lived on the coastal lowlands with the white people.

Palmer started the negotiations and, through his interpretors, offered the usual round of compliments to each of the head men and gifts that included tobacco. It was hard to tell what effect this had, for the Indians could have been made from metal poured into icy molds. Palmer acknowledged tactfully that the Indians had suffered abuses, just as they had transgressed against the whites. So the past would be forgiven, with nobody held to account for what had been done by either side. And it was the wish of the great white father to provide a new home for his red children away from this land where it seemed impossible for them to live in peace.

John said nothing, and Enos said nothing, and none of the entourage stirred.

The superintendent could add little beyond reminding John that he had signed the Lane treaty three years before, agreeing to go on the Table Rock reserve. This he had broken, whatever the excusing circumstances, and a great chief honored his word. Yet Indian honor could be redeemed, even yet, if all arms were surrendered, with the hostile bands coming to Fort Orford for transportation by sea to the new reservation at Yaquina Bay. If this was done, they would be given protection from the settlers they had wronged. Food, blankets and new clothing would be given them immediately from a supply train that even now was coming from Port Orford. If they agreed, there would be a great feast and many more gifts.

John and his lieutenants continued to sit impassively, but Luke noticed that some of the coast Indians showed interest. They began to talk among themselves. This was fairly calm, at first, but when the voices rose in intensity, Buchanan tactfully interrupted, suggesting that they discuss the matter in privacy, at their own camps, and return on the morrow with their answers. Since this seemed to head off an explosive row among the Indians, themselves, the command breathed a sigh of relief.

When the Indians had left the flat, the command divided itself quickly between two opinions. To some the apparent wavering in the coast Indians had been significant. "Hell, boys, if they cave in, what hope's John got of standing us off with what he'd have left to fight with?" Some of this mind even offered to bet on it, and they found plenty of takers. The majority opinion was that the impressive John had only come to the flat to estimate the force concentrated here and figure a way to fight it. So the day ended, and sentries walked uneasy posts through another long night, yet nothing went wrong. That fact alone restored some of the fading confidence in the optimists. The command got through breakfast and policed the big camp and had hardly finished when the Indians returned.

This time Colonel Buchanan took over, and he pressed hard, for he now read a more open susceptibility in the coast Indians than he had seen there the day before, and he had persuaded Palmer that it had become a strictly military situation. Briskly, Buchanan set the date for the proposed surrender as May 26th, the fourth day thereafter. The place would be the big meadows on the Rogue, some five miles above the mouth of the Illinois. The Indians would appear there on that date and give up their arms or—Buchanan now grew threatening—the enormous forces above and below them would crush them in the heart of the gorge.

Glancing at John, finally, the colonel said, "So far in the powwow, the big chief has not spoken. What is in his heart about this?"

Luke had a feeling that Buchanan's threat had undone anything the more gentle Palmer had accomplished the day before. For a moment after the translation, John only stared at the colonel. Then he rose slowly to his feet. He looked tired, even weak, yet from the hushed way the other Indians waited, Luke knew that they were still under his control, that John's answer would decide the issue for all of them.

When John spoke his voice was like the rumble of low thunder. His eyes were on Buchanan, the white man's warrior, and not on Palmer, the man of peace. "You are a great chief," he said. "So am I a great chief."

After the interpreter's translation, Buchanan nodded his agreement.

John made a sweeping motion with his arm, and his heart

seemed to swell with fury. He spoke loudly, pausing only to let the interpreter convey his words on to listening white ears. "This is my country. I was in it when these trees were very little, not higher than my head. My heart is sick fighting the whites, but I want to live in my country." He paused after this translation for several breaths. "I will not go out of my country. I will, if the whites are willing, go back to my old country on the Applegate and live as I used to do among the whites. They can visit my camp, and I will visit their camps. But I will not lay down my arms and go on a new reserve in a strange land. I will not go back to the old reserve." He shook his head. "No! I will fight!"

In the hushed aftermath, Luke knew that a voice had spoken to them out of the ages, a voice that had crossed the lips of the unvanquished many times in history. The insight, which all seemed to share, dignified the moment. The hush lingered while the Indians filed off into the timber.

Turning to the superintendent with an uneasy laugh, Buchanan said, "I'm glad he hasn't got followers worthy of him, Mr. Palmer."

Skeptically, Palmer said, "You still think the others will cave in?"

"By the 26th," Buchanan said with assurance. "That's why I allowed them four days more. He's fired them up for the moment, but it won't last, Mr. Palmer."

The colonel's confidence was unshakeable, and he began at once to prepare for the surrender. Smith's company was ordered to the big meadows above the Y to receive the Indians when they came in to give up their arms. Luke was assigned to him to acquaint the the captain with that vicinity. Jones was stationed at the mouth of the Illinois, five miles below where Smith would be, to seal off the tributary river. Augur's company and the Gold Beach Guards were ordered to proceed a few miles down the Sebastopol trail to clear away brush that choked much of the riverbank route, opening it for the passage of the large band of Indians. Buchanan would set up his command post at Augur's camp, and he invited Palmer to be his guest there while they waited. Finally, Reynolds' company was sent off to meet the supply train so that the promised feast and gifts could be given the Indians as promised.

Smith's company was the first to leave Oak Flat. Being dismounted except for a few pack horses and under heavy knapsacks and blanket rolls, it experienced slow going on up the Rogue to the assigned station. The section they eventually reached, however, was as beautiful as it was lonely, forest slopes coming down to its open carpet of grass. The area did not seem hemmed in, for narrow bays cut into the the mountains, from which came cold clear streams to flow across the meadow to the river. Smith chose one of these streams, on the north side of the Rogue, an open expanse where he could not be come upon by surprise. There he set up camp and mounted the howitzer.

Luke was glad to be with this company, and not only because it was the forefront of what was now a scattered army force. Andrew Jackson Smith was the only officer in Buchanan's command with a long and first-hand experience with the Rogue Indians. Out of the military academy at West Point some eighteen years, he had built Fort Lane four years ago and had commanded it ever since. Frequent contacts had given Luke an acquaintance that had now ripened to a real friendship.

By the fire, that evening, Luke voiced the doubts that haunted his mind. "Seems to me the colonel's takin' a mighty long chance scatterin' out this way on nothin' but his hunch. Jones is five miles below us, Augur eight or ten below him. Reynolds is off with the supply train, wherever it is now. A real handy setup if the Injuns come out of the gorge with their hands up. But not so good if they come out fightin'."

Switzer, Hagen and Underwood, Smith's lieutenants, were at the same fire, and they seemed to share Luke's uneasiness. Smith poked up the fire, then said hesitantly, "It's a gamble, but not as looping as it looks. I was told this in confidence by the colonel, but it might make you feel easier. A despatch went to General Lamerick by way of Crescent City as soon as the council date was set. He's supposed to be moving down on the renegades by now. The colonel thinks that'll tip the balance and drive them out to us."

"If Lamerick does move," Luke commented.

"Yes."

"And then the Injuns might not come out so peaceable."

"No," Smith agreed. "Not necessarily."

18   EACH OF THE DAYS that had to pass before the fateful May 26th was a ratchet that tightened the nerves of the eighty-odd men and officers on the big meadow. They were all restless and had a natural instinct to explore their surroundings, but Smith kept a tight rein on them, holding them in camp. Then, on the last day before the big one, the fair weather that had lightened the discomforts broke abruptly.

The sky opened to release a mountain downpour that doused the cookfires and soaked the blankets and drenched the un-sheltered command to the skin.

So the day of the scheduled surrender dawned in too much misery for anybody to grow as excited as they had all expected to be. In the night the storm had blown inland, but clothing and fuel were sodden, and it was hard even to get fires going briskly enough to fry bacon and boil coffee. In midmorning the sun came out and began to steam away the moisture, but noon passed with no sign of the hostiles. It began to look as if the Indians were going to wait in the stronghold to be rooted out. Nobody this close to the lair was eager for such an undertaking.

Then, in midafternoon, excitement gusted through the camp. It began as a yell when somebody noticed three In-dians, displaying a white flag, off on the upstream edge of the meadow.

"Hey! There they are!"

But there were those three Indians and no more. They were motioned to come forward, and a detail went out to meet them. Escorted to where Smith waited, the Indians in-formed him that they had been sent by John, who knew Smith would respect a flag of truce. The Indians would be in but not until the next day, the emissaries reported, for the gorge trails had been slickened treacherously by the down-pour, and three-fourths of the bands were women, children and oldsters.

Luke felt relief, although it amazed him that in spite of that fiery speech at the council John had decided to give up, and he saw an even more open relief in the faces of the others who listened, including Smith's. The couriers were given food and then were permitted to leave with Smith's reply that the delay was understood. Afterward a man could be heard whistling cheerily now and then. Supper was cooked and eaten, and in the dusk Luke heard a harmonica playing off somewhere in the distance.

The interlude of relaxation was not to be long, for dark-ness had hardly closed in when another courier arrived. This one was a lone Indian who said he had come in secret from the camp of Tyee George, a subchief in the stronghold. John's communication, according to George, was a trick in-tended to throw Smith off guard. The fiery old chief was aware of how recklessly Buchanan had scattered his troops in his overconfidence. He believed himself capable of taking them on unit by unit, with Smith's to be the first. But the coast Indians were truly in favor of surrendering, with George's own inclinations leaning that way.

When this runner had been taken off to be fed, Luke said laconically, "That makes more sense to me than John's trucklin' to the colonel. Which one you gonna believe, Captain?"

"You know which I'd rather," Smith said. "Not, however, that I trust either one. That speech of John's at the council sent shivers up my back. He could be behind both messages, trying to make us squirm. On the other hand, George could have decided that their cause is lost and is trying to curry favor with us."

"So what do you do?"

"Hope for the best and prepare for the worst," Smith answered.

"Gonna send for reinforcements?"

"Not till this is clarified. The whole idea could be to create confusion."

East of the bivouac and on the north edge of the big meadow, a low ridge rose between two small creeks that ran across to the river. Smith ordered camp struck at once, and in hardly more than an hour had moved to that position. The elevated ground the company then occupied was of no great height and barely twenty feet wide. But it extended for a distance of some two hundred and fifty yards and thus accommodated the command in a position suitable for a fight. The small streams at either base could furnish abundant water.

By morning Smith was convinced that something unwelcome was being prepared by the Indians. Tearing a leaf from his notebook, he addressed a message to Colonel Buchanan, reporting that the Indians had not come in and mentioning the conflicting messages received from them. Since the route down the river was easy to follow, Smith sent off a corporal with the despatch, keeping Luke on hand.

That step was taken in the nick of time. The corporal had hardly disappeared at the lower end of the meadow when an innocent-looking mound, north of Smith's ridge and between it and the mountainside, erupted in massive rifle fire. Bullets cut through the scubby growth about the command, bringing down a shower of leaves, to answer the question of which Indian message had been truthful.

Smith barked orders that his officers relayed, and the command sprinted to positions from which to return fire. While some of the men shot at the little smoke blossoms above the mound, others scooped out more rifle pits, and Smith had the howitzer turned on the mound. In a moment the air between mound and ridge, crisscrossed by bullets, was also jarred by the field piece. Luke found himself in a rifle pit, his civilian status notwithstanding, for this was every man's fight for his life.

It was soon apparent that the Indian shooting was more effective than that of the command for the simple reason that the hostiles' weapons were newer and of longer range. John had shrewdly exploited that fact when he chose his position, to which he had brought his braves by slipping along the timbered mountainside. From the outcries about him, Luke knew there had been casualties on the ridge already.

Yet Smith's coolness was impressive. He could not tell yet how great was the strength John had managed to bring against him, but his own flanks and rear were still open to attack, if there were other war parties near. So while he tried to offset his inferior firearms by whacking howitzer shells into the Indian position, Smith prepared another message. This one was to be carried to Jones, lying on the Illinois and the nearest available help.

His second courier had not left the ridge when a party of some forty Indians, who had slipped down along the river unseen, came howling toward the ridge from the rear. Smith yelled to Lieutenant Hagen to swing the howitzer around, and he reversed part of the skirmish line to help break up the charge. But the Indians hesitated when they saw the big gun, and before it could be fired they had taken cover. Other Indians were coming from the river brush behind them, and these fanned out on the flanks of the first party. The command knew it was cut off, then, by a force three times its own size. It had fallen to these eighty, out of some twelve hundred men marshaled against the Indians since the break from the reservation, to have it out with them.

Luke was not long in recognizing the voice he heard frequently above the roar of battle as that of John, who seemed to be directing operations from the north mound. Guided by this carrying voice, the Indians, around ten o'clock, built up the shooting from that angle to a blistering intensity. Following this, the warriors on the meadow made a mass charge toward Smith's ridge, coming from all directions. Officers and noncoms snapped orders all along the skirmish lines. Yet the command scarcely needed orders to pour out the fiercest fire yet. When the howitzer was added to that hail of death, the Indians on the flat turned back.

Lieutenant Switzer crawled up to Luke, scrubbed a hand over his smeary face and said, "That fellow John could make army officers I've known look like duffers at a shooting gallery. He's handling his people like he'd commanded troops all his life."

"What's he cost us?" Luke asked.

"Nineteen casualties, so far," Switzer said grimly. "It's going higher."

There was indeed a skilled pattern to the Indian attack, and Luke saw it repeated through the afternoon. There would be a sudden onslaught of long-range fire from the mound that was John's command post. Then, from the flat, would come a charge, sometimes in mass, again by small parties that tried to scale the steeper and more weakly defended sections of Smith's ridge. Time and again these were barely beaten back.

So the long day ended with no sign of reinforcements from down the river. The Indians on the meadow withdrew for the night, but the north mound remained occupied and busy. The command knew that John did not mean to let it make an escape in the darkness, so it set to work to improve its defenses. A few men slipped down to the creeks for water and made it back. By then the casualties stood at twenty-two. It grew evident that the message to Buchanan had not reached him.

The attack was renewed at daylight. and now John pressed hard for a victory before help could come for Smith. Somehow Smith countered his every move and somehow he beat it back. The howitzer ammunition shrank, and around noon it ran out. At four o'clock the casualties stood at twenty-nine, over a third of the command, and by then even small arms ammunition was scarce.

Only minutes after four o'clock, the big voice of John rang over the field once more. It was soon clear what the order had been. True to the established pattern, a rain of bullets came from the north mound, where the sharpshooters seemed to have inexhaustible ammunition. Smith realized that the Indians were forming en masse on both his flanks. He could see the dark figures dart through the cover, and he knew that John wanted a decision before another sundown. Smith crawled along his lines, encouraging his men. Without the howitzer, their chances of beating off another massed assault were poor, and everyone knew it as well as John did.

John's final words of command were drowned in a new and wholly unexpected sound. At the lower end of the meadow a bugle gave voice, and the men swiveled their heads to see figure upon figure spew onto the flat, clad in the uniform of the army. The men on the ridge rent the abrupt silence with cheers. They rose up to join the charge on the Indians who found themselves caught between the two commands.

Orders from the mound poured out in the Indian tongue. It was plain that they were futile orders, for the Indians for the first time rattled and broke. Now they fought only to disengage themselves and make for the narrow portals of the upper gorge. A running fight raged far up the river, but the Indians, minus casualties that proved to have been extreme, made their escape into the stronghold.

Only then did Smith's command learn of the chain of misadventures that had nearly brought this help too late. Following down the north side of the river, the corporal despatched with the message to Buchanan had seen no one from Jones' command, which was on the other side and at some distance up the Illinois. Hurrying on, he had found that Buchanan, with Augur's company and the Gold Beach Guards, had worked well down the river in their brush chopping and were eighteen miles below the ridge on which Smith lay under attack.

But the corporal had reached Buchanan's shifting command post at last. Since Smith had reported only that the Indians had not come in and there was a chance that he would be attacked, the colonel had returned the messenger to inquire whether Smith thought he should be reinforced. So the hapless noncom turned about, and when he reached Big Meadows again it was to find that Smith was already under attack, surrounded, with no possibility of reaching him. The courier had already covered thirty-six miles on foot, but once more he turned about. Yet night was soon upon him and before long he was lost. Falling exhausted, he slept until daylight, and then made his way again to Buchanan.

John's final gamble had been valiant, and he had nearly won it, but not quite. For against him stood his equal, a frontier army captain with eighty seasoned men. It was soon evident from the casualties found on the flat that Smith had shot away John's fighting muscle. Proof of this came during the next three days in which Indians, singly and in groups, slipped out of the gorge to surrender. On the third day George and Limpy appeared and gave up their arms. On the fourth, Major Latshaw, from Lamerick's command, emerged from the gorge to announce that the stronghold had been cleaned out.

Only John and Enos were missing, with a pitiful handful of their most loyal followers. They were helpless, harmless renegades now, to be hunted and run down or to be brought by their own hopeless situation to surrender.

On the first day of June, Luke rode into the rejoicing town of Sebastopol. The news of the climatic battle had reached it well ahead of him, although the army was still mopping up in the field. He came by the old Johnson place without seeing Jody, yet he supposed that was just as well. The trouble was settled, and Gold Beach was free to return to normal life. That meant the ranch for him, which he must restore. For Carol's home, as well as his, and he wondered why there was none of Sebastopol's joy in his own heart.

Before going down to the family camp to claim Carol, he stopped at his own place. Jody wasn't there, either, yet Murphy was on hand. The big Irishman had an odd light in his eyes when they shook hands, and Luke said at once, "Where's Jody?"

"Around somewhere," Murphy said vaguely and shrugged.

Luke washed the trail dust from his face, in no hurry to go on to his betrothed. Jody still did not show up, and at last Murphy said in open embarrassment, "Well, Luke, there's somethin' I gotta tell you that I don't relish."

Luke's only thought was of Jody, and his throat tightened, "Bad?"

"Well—sad. A thing like that always is, no matter who it happens to. But I don't reckon it's bad, Luke—not if what I figure about you is right. Carol Dennis ain't around any more. She cleared out the night word come that the Injuns had been whipped. Or she tried to, that is."

What Murphy went on to say was incredible, yet Luke knew that it fit everything he had come instinctively to know about Carol. She had strung Pete Latta along for quite a while, Jody had told Murphy afterward. That was why she and Jody had fallen out. A couple of homeguards had cleared up the rest after they'd been arrested for accepting bribes.

"From Carol?" Luke gasped.

Murphy nodded. "Usin' Latta's gold dust."

At first Latta had been the army's prisoner, held to be tried when he could be turned over to the civil authorities. But when the army left for the mountains, the gambler was placed in the custody of the small detachment of home guard left at Sebastopol. Everyone knew he must have had a big stash of gold dust. Carol had managed somehow to talk with him and persuade him to tell her where it was hidden. Using part of the gold and her own charms, she had bought

Latta's release and a couple of militia horses on which to make their escape.

"They got as far as the Chetco," Murphy concluded. "Abbott's volunteers, down there, found their bodies beside the trail."

Luke shut his eyes for a moment, but all he felt was what Murphy had called it. A sadness. Then he turned and saw Jody coming up the trail from the south. She had seen him and was half-running. He went hurrying to meet her.

Chad Merriman was the pseudonym Giff Cheshire used for his first novel, *Blood on the Sun*, published by Fawcett Gold Medal in 1952. He was born in 1905 on a homestead in Cheshire, Oregon. The county was named for his grandfather who had crossed the plains in 1852 by wagon from Tennessee and the homestead was the same one his grandfather had claimed upon his arrival. Cheshire's early life was colored by the atmosphere of the Old West which in the first decade of the century had not yet been modified by the automobile. He attended public schools in Junction City and, following high school, enlisted in the U.S. Marine Corps and saw duty in Central America. In 1929 he came to the Portland area in Oregon and from 1929 to 1943 worked for the U.S. Corps of Engineers. By 1944, after moving to Beaverton, Oregon, he found he could make a living writing Western and North-Western short fiction for the magazine market and presently stories under the byline Giff Cheshire began appearing in *Lariat Story Magazine, Dime Western,* and *North-West Romances*. His short story *Strangers in the Evening* won the Zane Grey Award in 1949. Cheshire's Western fiction was characterized from the beginning by a wider historical panorama of the frontier than just cattle ranching and frequently the settings for his later novels are in his native Oregon. *Thunder on the Mountain* (1960) focuses on Chief Joseph and the Nez Perce war, while *Wenatchee Bend* (1966) and *A Mighty Big River* (1967) are among his best-known titles. However, his Chad Merriman novels for Fawcett Gold Medal remain among his most popular works, notable for their complex characters, expert pacing, and authentic backgrounds.